Exiled

A Return of the Elves Novella

D1305997

Bethany Adams

Exiled
A Return of the Elves Novella
by Bethany Adams

First Edition

This book is a work of fiction and does not represent any
individual, living or dead. Names, characters, places, and
incidents either are products of the author's imagination or
are used fictionally.

Edited by Jody Wallace at www.jodywallace.com
Cover art by Eve Milady at http://venetian-eve.tumblr.com
Interior Design by Gaynor Smith of Indie Books Gone Wild
www.ibgw.net

Published in the United States of America

Acknowledgements

As always, I'd like to thank my family for all of their patience and support. I couldn't do it without you.

Huge thanks to each and every reader. I've received so many nice reviews and messages, and I can't even tell you how much they mean to me. Thank you!

Thank you to Jessica and Natasha for being such awesome critique partners. And for putting up with me! :)

To Jody and Eve for your amazing work and unerring support. I wouldn't be where I am without your awesomeness.

I'd also like to give a big thanks to L. Nahay for pointing out my little naming issue. I hope this is better. :)

To everyone who has taken a chance

on my humble work.

Your support means the world.

1

Inona scowled at the stone arch, but her steps didn't falter as she strode toward the portal. Of all the duties assigned to her, this was her least favorite. Checking on the exiles. A bunch of wastrels, for the most part. She tugged uneasily at the odd, flimsy T-shirt, so thin she couldn't even conceal a knife beneath it. At least her thick blue pants had suitable pockets. Really, humans gave too little thought to protection.

Most of them.

With a wave to the portal guard, Inona marched straight through the invisible barrier to the Veil. The mists closed around her, and her insides gave a sick lurch at the tumultuous energy buffeting her. She rubbed her hand across her stomach. The Veil had grown worse since her last trip from Moranaia to Earth. Strands of color whirled as though tossed by a gale, and the one she sought, the one that would guide her to her destination, slipped away several times before she grasped it with her magic.

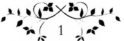

Latching tightly, Inona tugged with her power, a soft *whoosh* hissing through her lips as she slipped across boundless space. She swallowed against a rush of nausea. Gods, this was rougher than it should have been. Her eyes squeezed closed as the energy buffeted her, almost as though it wanted to shake her loose. It was like trying to cross flood-swelled rapids instead of a calm stream.

As she neared her destination, she grasped for the sub-strand that would take her to the exit she needed. Finally, Inona stumbled through the other side of the portal. She reached out to steady herself against the nearby rock and blinked against the shift in light. The small crevice in the side of the bluff hid her from view, but it didn't block the afternoon sun.

Inona leaned back against the warm stone to catch her breath. The last time she'd been through here, the area had been sparsely populated. How many Earth years had passed since then? Frowning, she did a quick calculation. At least eleven, she thought, though she was no expert at time conversion. That was long enough for the humans to have built their settlements closer to the ridge.

Bracing herself, Inona peeked around the edge of the crevice. To the left, the land sloped upward. Trees swayed in the breeze and birds chirped softly. Just as she remembered. She glanced right, down the hill curving away from the base of the bluff. Then she cursed. A neighborhood had sprung up near the bottom, the tidy human houses replacing the forest that had once reigned. She'd have to be more careful now.

She ducked back and pulled a scrap of paper from her pocket. With a scowl, she scanned the list of names. Only three this time, but she hadn't met the first one before. *Delbin Rayac, formerly of Oria.* Coric had been responsible for him the last couple of centuries, but the dubious honor had passed to Inona while Coric and his wife welcomed their first child.

Inona sighed. Well, anything for a new parent.

Delbin's eyes locked onto his target.

"You!" he said from his perch, the microphone in his mask carrying his words wide. The blond on the other side of the dirt clearing gave him an uneasy glance and walked faster. "I know you heard me, lady. I'm louder than that ugly orange shirt you're wearing. Did your husband actually let you leave the house that way?"

She froze, her body stiffening. Finally, she turned to glare at him. "I don't have a husband."

"Wife, then?" he asked, winking. "I don't judge."

"Yeah, right," the woman muttered, so softly a human wouldn't have heard.

But he wasn't human. "Yeah, I'm not buying it either," Delbin said. Then he smirked, though she wouldn't be able to see it through his mask. "Anyway, you're too ugly for either one."

Her mouth opened on a gasp, and for the first time, her gaze shifted to the target next to his tank. Delbin swished his toes through the water. *She definitely wants to dunk me.* But

that wasn't what she really needed. He sent out a tendril of energy, connecting to her mind with the lightest of touches.

"This guy doesn't know what he's talking about. I'm beautiful," Delbin sent into her thoughts.

The woman's shoulders straightened, and she shot him a haughty scowl. "Pick on someone else."

Delbin called out another half-hearted insult as she marched toward the Ferris wheel, but his job was done. Not that Grunge would agree. But if the dunk tank's profits dipped a little when Delbin was in charge, the old man would have to deal. Destroying people for money would never be his thing.

Sighing, Delbin slipped his fingers beneath his mask and wiped away the sweat. The mask was way too hot to wear in the heat of a Tennessee fall, but with the insults he delivered, the garish clown disguise had saved him from more than one beating. Since they'd started this fair circuit, he'd had quite a few threats from men who didn't like having their masculinity called into question.

Grunge ambled up, his steel-gray hair sticking up at even odder angles than usual. The state of the old man's hair was a running joke among the crew. "How many dunks ya got?" he grumbled.

"Two," Delbin answered. "But the day's still young."

Grunge nodded his head toward a tall man entering through the front gate. "How about that'n?"

An odd one for this area. Delbin's eyes narrowed, taking in the long black hair tied away from the man's face and the arrogant tilt of his chin. *Really odd.* Delbin started to send

out his energy to test the newcomer but froze as the tip of the man's ear peeked through his hair. Pointed. So he was an elf—or maybe one of the Sidhe. Could he be from Moranaia? The guy didn't look like any of the guides who'd checked on Delbin before.

"Not him," Delbin finally answered.

"Ah, come on." Smirking, Grunge slapped a hand against the side of the tank. "He's full of himself. Probably make us rich trying to dunk ya."

"Looks more likely to knife me in an alley, old man," Delbin said, careful to keep his tone light though his insides twisted.

Dark energy swirled around the elf, so thick even the humans gave him a wide berth. Delbin swallowed hard. Then almost sagged in relief at the sight of the three college boys eyeing the dunk tank. He shifted on his perch and focused on the trio. Whatever the elf was doing, Delbin wanted no part of it.

He straightened on his perch and called out the next insult.

Inona stared, mouth gaping, at the odd array of metal structures and flashing lights. What *was* this place? She tightened her hand around the small beacon stone, but the slim tendril of energy didn't waver. Delbin Rayac was definitely here. She ground her teeth as a wave of cheering washed over her, punctuated by shouts and screams. Humans were *everywhere*. This was how he remained inconspicuous?

Had Coric known their exile would be in such a crowded place?

A sudden breeze whipped around Inona, cooling the sweat coating her shirt after her long walk. With the wind came a blend of scents she had no words to describe. Sweet, spicy, tangy, savory—those she knew. But what kinds of foods produced such an odd mix? She scanned the crowd beyond the gate and spotted a small girl eating some kind of blue, fuzzy stuff atop a conical piece of paper. Surely that wasn't supposed to be edible?

Inona's gaze landed on the blinking sign atop the gate. *Wilde's Traveling Fair.* A traveling fair? Despite visiting the modern human world quite often, she still thought of wagons and tents when she heard that word. She scanned the hulking metal structures, many with moving parts. Giant cups spun in circles or whooshed up and down artificial hills. There was even a giant wheel with dangling seats. Definitely not like the carnivals of old with their daring performers and strange menageries.

"Are you going in or not?" a voice called, and Inona focused on a human girl hefting a garbage bag from a nearby can.

Inona jerked her head in a quick nod. "Yes, sorry. This place is quite a sight."

"Just the way Grunge likes it," the human said, a cheerful, affectionate lilt to her voice.

Forcing a smile, Inona nodded again. "Can't wait."

Ah, curses. Her golden skin grew hot as she ambled toward the ticket booth. Inona hadn't been caught gawking

6

at anything in years, and attracting such notice could be a costly mistake in such a busy place. But she couldn't stress about it now. She did her best to shove her embarrassment aside as she dug a hand into her pocket for a slip of human money.

"Ten dollars gets you in, plus two free rides," an adolescent male announced from his seat in the ticket booth, his attention focused on a shiny rectangle in his hand. "Twenty gets you a two-hour pass. Thirty for rides all day."

"I'm not here for the rides," Inona answered as she sorted through the numbered papers.

His gaze darted to her face at the sound of her voice, and his eyes went wide. "Okay. Umm…"

Inona handed him a piece of money with *10* on the corner and let him place a paper bracelet around her wrist. Was this some form of human security? She grinned at the thin blue strip, and the boy jerked back, his throat bobbing in a gulp. Her smile widened at his lusty stare.

Too old for you, she thought. She gave a jaunty wave as she turned to merge with the crowd. *Centuries too old.*

Tinny music, excited voices, and the plaintive cry of a child flowed around her. Inona grinned at the young boy who'd plopped himself in the dirt, his small finger jutting toward a display of toy cars at a booth. Her younger brother had done something similar at his first Midsummer festival. *And* his second. The tension in her shoulders relaxed at the memory. Some things spanned worlds.

She'd have to remind him of that next time he gave her grief for leaving the plains.

A sharp crack, followed by a splash and loud cheering, caught Inona's attention. But something in the sounds gave Inona pause, a tone in the shouts not matching the celebratory air of the place. Her hand drifted to the knife concealed in her pocket as she searched the area for the source. And…there. A clump of young men slapped hands and bumped fists around a square booth with a cage around the top.

A cage?

Inona started forward, only to pause a few paces away as a man levered himself onto a small seat behind the bars. Water plastered his clothes to his body and caressed the hard, muscled lines of his forearms. Involuntarily, Inona licked her lips. Then her gaze reached his face, and she gasped, her heart giving a thud.

Huge, red lips. Pointed teeth. Wild colors ringing the eyes. Perhaps there was a reason for the cage.

Her fingers curled around the hilt of her knife, ready to yank it from its hidden pocket. If the humans couldn't eliminate this threat, she certainly could. But then the deformed man shook his head, flinging drops from his puffy blue hair, and slipped a finger beneath the edge of his skin. Inona squinted, and a chuckle escaped when she realized he wore a mask. Whatever horror the humans had based *that* face on she didn't want to see.

The worst part of the job is getting dunked, Delbin reflected. Oh, the breeze drifting over his wet clothes cooled him for

a moment. Then the humidity joined in on the fun, and the fabric strangled his limbs and chafed at his skin. He grimaced beneath his mask as the group of laughing teens sauntered away, calling out taunts. Then he heaved out a sigh and started searching the crowd for his next target.

At the edge of the small clearing, a woman caught his eye. Her hair was almost as honey-gold as her skin, an unusual combination here. Most of the humans with skin that tone had dark hair. Delbin's attention drifted down to her tight T-shirt and snug jeans. Leanly muscled, curved just right... *Damn.* She could stand there and try to dunk him all day.

"Hey, lady," he called, and her gaze snapped to his. "Out here for a good time?"

With children present, Delbin had to be careful with his insults, but he could tell she hadn't missed the suggestive lilt in his voice. Her face reddened, and her lips thinned into a straight line. As usual, he released a discreet tendril of magic, searching for a weakness he could help her overcome. The best part of his job.

Until his magic encountered her shielding. Her eyes flared with fury and power at his attempted intrusion, and Delbin froze. *Shitfuckdamn.* She wasn't human. How had he not noticed? She heaved a breath, and his glance returned to her chest. He winced ruefully beneath his mask. That was how. Dammit, he knew better than to let himself be so distracted.

With his attention on the female elf, the sharp rap on the side of the tank took him by surprise. "Shift's over," Grunge called.

For once, that announcement didn't fill him with relief. The woman stared at him as he spun on his seat, and her attention hadn't shifted after he'd climbed down and peeked around the side. Not good. He wasn't supposed to do magic around humans, and the hard glint in her eyes told him she knew it. Was she from Moranaia?

The man he'd seen before flickered in his memory. What were the chances of seeing two non-humans in less than an hour? The guides in charge of exiles rarely traveled in pairs, and in all his time on the circuit, Delbin had encountered fae or half-blood beings only a handful of times. Most of them had been *with* the fairs. Or running them, like Grunge.

Unease settling in his stomach, he ducked around the back edge of the dunk tank. He gave a quick nod to Grunge and Charlie, a six-foot giant of a man who made sure Bozos like Delbin weren't attacked on the way to the employee tents. He didn't turn to look at the woman, though his shoulders tightened against her gaze as it bore into his back. With the other two men there, she wouldn't dare approach. Nor would the few people who tossed glares his way when they recognized him from the dunk tank.

He'd just have to hope she wouldn't be able to identify him without the mask.

2

The stone heated in Inona's hand as the man's magic hit her shields, identifying him as her target. Glaring at his back as he strode away, she muttered a curse. Oh, she'd found her exile, all right. *Casually using his magic on others.* Coric wouldn't have let that stand. Delbin might have gone renegade in the couple of years since his last check, she supposed, but there'd been no indication from Coric that Delbin was at risk of such behavior.

Could it have been a fluke?

Inona forced an easy expression across her face and ambled along the aisle, pretending interest in the booths and rides she passed. She didn't need to follow her prey too closely, not with the tracking stone. If he realized that she'd been sent to check on him and tried to leave, she'd know. As fit as he clearly was, he couldn't outrun her. And *she* wasn't forbidden from using magic against him, so long as the humans didn't notice.

At the far end of the midway, he ducked into a large tent set over to the side. Trying to blend in while she watched for him, Inona purchased one of the colorful, fluff-topped cones. Then she settled at a nearby table and examined the odd treat. Most of the people she'd seen had picked small pieces off the top to eat, so she did the same.

Inona gasped as sweetness burst across her tongue. Gods, too much. She swallowed hard, her eyes watering, and wished devoutly for something to drink. Ale. Anything. Had the humans extracted the very nectar of the plants and condensed it into…this? She glanced around for a garbage can. Humans might give this stuff to children, but *she* didn't have to eat it.

So much for blending in.

As Inona tossed the blue nectar-fuzz into a partially filled can, an odd shiver traced through her. She stilled, trying to identify the source. Her shielding was intact, and when she took a cautious glance around, she saw nothing but the human crowd. Yet the air vibrated with a sudden charge, a dark energy wafting around her from a point beyond the large tent.

Not Delbin. The tendril of power he'd sent her way hadn't felt anything like this. Swallowing hard, Inona grasped the hilt of her knife once more. She gathered her power, glanced around to make sure no one was watching, and cast a simple camouflage spell. It wouldn't hide her for long from the person wielding such dark magic, but it allowed her to creep around the edge of the stall next to the tent without being seen by humans. She hoped.

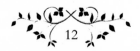

Delbin tossed a wave over his shoulder and pulled open the back entrance to the staff tent. He'd peeked out the front, only to find the woman throwing a ball of cotton candy into the trash. Her continued presence could be a coincidence, but he wasn't betting on it. Good thing there was more than one way in. The corner of his mouth tipped up as he secured the flap shut and turned toward the row of travel trailers at the back edge of the field.

Only to stop short at the sight of the man leaning on a tree a few paces away. The same guy he'd seen earlier.

Oh, shit. Delbin halted, barely managing to suppress a shudder as a wave of dark energy pulsed from the other elf. For elf he was, making no attempt to hide the points of his ears beneath his long black hair. He hadn't appeared to notice Delbin before, but clearly he had. The elf smiled widely as he strode forward.

"What a pleasure to see one of my brethren," the stranger said, his voice smooth and pleasant. At least on the surface. "Might I have the honor of an introduction?"

Every hair on Delbin's body rose despite the surface courtesy of the request. Something was wrong here. Very wrong. Non-humans traveling or living on Earth almost universally kept a low profile. Even now, only a handful of fae worked at Grunge's fair, and none of them were open about it to humans. This was far from normal.

"I could ask the same. Fair patrons are not supposed to be back here."

"Ah, yes. Rules." The elf's smirk widened. "I am Moranai Dakiorn i Kien Moreln nai Moranaia. Your future king."

Delbin's heart slammed hard at the soft words. Kien, the exiled prince? He'd been kicked out of Moranaia a good century before Delbin. But Kien had used the title *Dakiorn*, second son and heir to the king. Had things changed on their home world in the last couple of years, or did the prince have some other agenda? Considering the type of energy in the air… *Yeah, I'm going with the second.*

"As much as anyone is my king here on Earth," Delbin finally said.

The prince's mouth pinched into a thin line. "You deny the dominion of the royal House?"

With a snort, Delbin shook his head. "I still follow our laws." *Mostly.* "But you know as well as I do that the people of Moranaia care little for exiles."

A harsh truth. Not even the brother Delbin had saved bothered to check on him. Prince Kien smirked again, and Delbin shoved aside the resentment toward his kin. He couldn't be distracted from someone so dangerous. Whatever the prince wanted, it almost certainly wasn't to reinforce the laws of Moranaia.

"I care," Kien said. "Join my group, and you'll have proof."

"What group is that?" a voice called, and both males spun toward the source.

The woman. Delbin almost groaned at the sight of her, standing tall by the corner with her hands shoved in her pockets. What was she doing? She wore a T-shirt and jeans, not armor. If she wasn't a mage, then she was vulnerable.

He opened his mouth to urge her to leave, but the prince's bark of laughter cut across the distance. The woman stood taller, her expression resolute.

"A guide so far from home," Prince Kien drawled. "You think to know my secrets? You may tell your lord, Lyrnis Dianore, that I'll find him soon enough."

She jerked her hands from her pockets, and Delbin's mouth fell open at the sight of the knives she'd pulled from...somewhere. "Not if I can help it."

Okay, maybe not vulnerable.

The prince chuckled. "I'll have to deal with you another time." His gaze flicked to Delbin. "And you. I'll find you again. Think on it."

As the woman charged forward, Prince Kien faded. Dissolved as though he'd never been. Delbin cursed. How had he been fooled by an illusion? With the strength of his mind magic, he could usually discern the lack of true presence. The prince must be able to project more than an image of his physical form. Had he even been in the crowd earlier, or had it all been fake?

Delbin released his power more freely than he normally would in the off chance he could trace Kien's energy. But he caught only a flicker disappearing beyond the back trailers. "Well, that was unusual," he said to the woman as she drew to a halt beside him.

"Delbin Rayac, it seems we need to talk." Her gaze flicked to the thin wall of the tent and then back. "In private."

Ah, hell, she knew his name. She really was a scout from Moranaia. But if she'd come to check on him, what about...

"Where is Coric? Did something happen to him?"

The woman blinked, forehead wrinkling at the urgency in his voice. "He's fine. He's on leave for the birth of his first child."

Delbin's breath left in a rush. *Thank the Gods.* Coric might have been tasked with keeping him in line, but he was Delbin's most steadfast friend. Only Coric and Lord Moren knew the truth of Delbin's exile. Then the rest of the woman's statement processed, and he smiled.

His first child. Coric and Fena had been hoping for a child for decades. He must be thrilled. "You'll have to take my congratulations back with you."

"You might have a chance to deliver them yourself," she grumbled, gesturing toward the travel trailers with the knife she held. "If you have one of those, let's go. I have to decide what to do with you."

That didn't sound good. Wincing, Delbin started across the clearing. "I recommend putting the blades away. We do have some security, you know."

Though she didn't answer, she did shove the knives back into her pockets as she strode beside him. How did she do it? There was no telltale bulge in the snug denim, no sign she could possibly be armed. Delbin ran his hand through his hair, a grudging smile slipping across his lips. Did she have other weapons concealed beneath her simple Earth clothes?

His gaze traveled, unbidden, along her body, before he wrenched his attention back to the huddled travel trailers. No use becoming interested in a Moranaian woman—especially not a guide who so clearly scorned him. Coric wouldn't have

shared Delbin's secrets, so there was no way for her to know why he'd been exiled. She would view him as a shirker or a lawbreaker, a person unworthy of Moranaia.

Delbin led her around the handful of trailers that blocked the bulk of the camp from fairgoer's eyes. Two of the small campers belonged to families, and a third was Grunge's. The largest was divided into small sleeping quarters. But Delbin hadn't liked those. Stifling a grin at the woman's pinched expression, he waved at the pair of workers eating lunch around a small campfire as he headed to the line of tents on the far side.

When he stopped at his tent, his smile finally slipped free. The incredulous look she turned on him was priceless.

"What's wrong?" he asked, trying for an innocent tone.

"I said more private," she snapped. She gestured sharply at the tent. "You know we can't talk freely here."

Well, he never had been particularly good at playing innocent. Shrugging, he pointed his thumb over his shoulder. "We can get in the truck."

"The..." Her gaze narrowed on the vehicle in question. He could practically see her analyzing the risk of being enclosed inside the cab versus the benefit of being able to question him without being overheard. Finally, she nodded. "Fine."

Heat rushed into Inona's cheeks as she tugged fruitlessly on the door handle. She'd been in human vehicles a handful of times while on missions, but those had been public

transport, all similar in design. All she'd had to do was pull up on the handle embedded in the door. Why wasn't that working this time?

She felt a tap on her shoulder and turned her head to see Delbin staring, one corner of his mouth twisted up in a half-smile. He lifted a small key ring and gave it a shake. "It's locked."

He leaned closer, and his chest brushed against her back as he slipped the key in its slot. Gods. It should have been an innocent action, but she couldn't stop a sudden surge of desire. A mutual one, if Delbin's swift inhale and sudden tension were anything to go by.

Her face flaming, Inona jerked to the side, away from his hold. She lifted her chin at the smug grin Delbin tossed her way. No way she was going to acknowledge what had happened. What was wrong with her, anyway? She couldn't afford to be attracted to another wastrel. One miscreant in her past was more than enough.

Delbin merely smirked at her and opened the rusty door, the squeal of metal on metal sounding around them. As he gave a flourishing wave toward the interior, Inona held her head high and plopped onto the cracked and crinkled leather of the seat. The door groaned again in complaint as he slammed it shut and rounded the front to the other side.

Only when they were completely enclosed did she turn to him. "This is where you live?"

"Pretty much," he answered, nodding cheerfully. He put the key its slot and turned. The engine roared to life, and blessedly cool air poured through panels in the dashboard.

"We travel all over the country, setting up our fair. The tent's mine, so I usually camp down south during the off-season."

She lifted a brow. "You spend that much time working?"

"Every day." The humor faded from his expression. "Tomorrow, we'll take down the rides and pack up for our next stop. It's a tough life, but good for someone different."

Inona stared at him. If he was willing to work, why hadn't he done so on Moranaia? He'd been listed as a shirker, refusing to contribute to society. Was he overstating the amount of effort the fair required? *Probably.* His lips shifted back into a smile, but a hint of sadness lingered in his light blue eyes.

She turned her gaze to the window. "You come from a good, hard-working family, always willing to—"

"You needn't bring them into this," Delbin growled. "I know what you think of me, but I won't explain myself to you. I don't even know your name."

"Inona," she answered. "Callian iy'dianore sonal i Inona Eman nai Braelyn."

"Well, Inona, are you planning to haul me back to Moranaia for my terrible crime?"

She blinked at the harsh, bitter tone of his words, such a contrast to the easygoing attitude he'd maintained so far. "That may not be necessary if you have a proper explanation for using your magic on humans."

A hint of his smirk returned. "Ah, but I didn't use it on a human. I used it on you."

"You—" Inona couldn't help it. She chuckled. He was a clever one, indeed. "I hope you don't expect me to believe that was a one-time thing."

Delbin ran his hand through his short blond hair. "Look, I'm not doing any harm. I haven't altered another's free will, and I haven't taken control of a single human. It's the merest brush of thought, no different than whispering into their ear."

She studied him for a moment. Was that a hint of red creeping up the back of his neck? "Why do you do it?"

"Some humans are too rough on themselves." At her questioning look, he shrugged. "Grunge has me working the dunk tank. My job is to call insults until the people passing by get angry enough to pay money for a chance to dunk me. And some people need that. They can defeat their enemy and feel good about themselves. But I can't let the ones who walk away just leave with my taunts in their heads."

For a moment, Inona couldn't speak. The sentiment was so...sweet. So different from what she would expect from an exile, a shirker. "You're using your magic to make people feel better about themselves?"

"It ought to be good for something," Delbin answered, and this time there was no mistaking the red staining his cheeks.

"Did Coric know about this?"

Delbin shook his head. "Last time he was here, I was in charge of the Ferris wheel."

"I see." She trailed her fingers over the bumpy dashboard in front of her as she considered what to do. He didn't seem to be doing any harm, and magic itself wasn't forbidden, so long as it was subtle, ethical, and necessary for survival. But why had he been speaking with the prince? "This doesn't explain your connection with Kien."

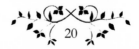

"I don't *have* a connection," Delbin said, lifting his hands. "I've never seen him before today."

"Really?" she demanded. "Seems like a huge coincidence."

He shifted to face her on the bench seat. "Last I heard, he'd been exiled to some remote dimension, but I stopped paying much attention to Moranaian news a while ago. Why did he call himself the heir to the throne?"

Inona's breath caught. "He *what?*"

"He called himself Dakiorn. Didn't you hear him?"

"*Miaran,*" she cursed. All of the scouts who traveled to Earth had been warned to watch out for Kien after he'd attempted to have Lord Lyr killed. But she wasn't high enough in rank to know the details. Was something else at play here? "I heard him say you should join his group. What do you know of it?"

Delbin leaned forward, his expression earnest. "Nothing. The energy around here has been odd for the last couple of years, but I had no clue there was any kind of group. What's going on?"

Should she tell him? Delbin could be lying about his involvement. He *had* been exiled, after all. But there was something about him that defied expectation and encouraged her to trust. What criminal or shirker went out of his way to make random strangers feel better about themselves? Nothing about this assignment made sense.

And if Delbin was innocent, then what did Kien want with him?

Resolved, Inona twisted sideways in her seat. "Kien sent an assassin against Lord Lyr. We've been warned to look out for him on missions to Earth."

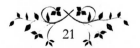

Delbin's brow creased. "Assassin? The portal to Moranaia is blocked for us exiles. What would be the point?"

"I don't know. I'm not in the Myern's confidence."

Silence fell. Expression thoughtful, Delbin tapped his fingers against his knee. Then movement in the window behind him caught her eye, and she opened her mouth to warn him just as a man with scraggly gray hair rapped his fist against the glass. Tensing, Delbin shifted around in his seat, then let out a laugh. He turned a knob on the side of the door, and the window lowered.

"Something wrong, Grunge?" Delbin asked.

"Need you to take tickets at the Tilt-A-Whirl," the older man said. "Meggie's girl got sick, so we're short-handed."

Delbin tossed a frown back at Inona. "What about my friend? She won't be here long, and I'd told her I'd have a break. Care if she tags along?"

"Nah, go ahead." Grunge gave her a wink. "She does any work, I'll pay her, too."

Before Inona could protest, he strode away, humming a lively tune. With a shrug, Delbin rolled up the window and turned off the truck. "You might as well go enjoy the fair while you figure out what to do with me. The Tilt-A-Whirl is a sight."

She wrapped her hand around his wrist, stopping him before he opened the door. "I won't turn you in for the way you used your magic," Inona said softly. "But I do need to stick around. I need to see what I can find out about Kien."

Delbin nodded. "I'll help."

An exile was offering to help? If he'd cared about Moranaia, wouldn't he have done anything in his power to stay there? But as he stared into her eyes, she found her head nodding in agreement. "Perhaps."

3

Excited shrieks filled the air as Delbin led Inona to the Tilt-A-Whirl. She looked pensive, a slight frown on her face as her gaze flicked around the fair. He could well imagine why. Moranaian festivals might have food and revelry, but they were nothing like this. No blinking lights or daredevil rides. And not nearly as many children, considering how much slower elves were to reproduce.

Then she turned her attention on him, and his heart gave an odd leap. Maybe she was wondering about him as well. He had seen on her face exactly what she thought of him—or he *had* been able to before their conversation in the truck. Moranaia was an amazing land. Basic needs were provided, including food and housing, to those willing to contribute. Exiles like him were rare, especially when banishment to Earth was the only other alternative.

Magic was so much weaker and less accessible here. Many of the shirkers didn't make it long.

But now…some of the scorn had faded from her eyes as she stared at him. Had she guessed there was more to him than his status might suggest? His lips tightened around the question. She'd better not guess. His absence kept his family safe. Too many questions could topple it all if rumors got back to Allafon.

"Do you sense something amiss?"

Delbin startled at her words. "No. Why do you ask?"

"You look like you're marching to your death, not a carnival ride," she answered wryly.

"Ah." He let out a laugh at that. She was perceptive. "I was thinking of my family. I rarely do."

Her steps slowed. "Why?"

"Why was I thinking of them? Or why do I rarely do so?" At her glance, he only smiled. "Seeing you made me wonder if they are well. My brother would be over a hundred now, and I've missed almost all of his life. I try not to think of loved ones I'll never be able to see."

"Your brother?" She did halt then, gripping his arm once more until he turned to face her. "The report I was given said nothing about a brother."

For a long moment, his head spun. Delbin forced himself to breathe. Not to react. "He was a child when I left. Perhaps his name wouldn't have been included."

"I…" Her shadowed gaze shifted away from his. "Perhaps."

She didn't believe it, and suddenly, Delbin wasn't so certain either. Had Allafon killed his brother after all?

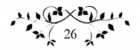

Had it all been for nothing? His shoulders slumped as the possibility flowed through him. Lord Moren had sworn his brother would be safe. What had gone wrong? Coric hadn't mentioned anything amiss.

"I'm sorry," Inona whispered. "I'll see what I can find out when I return."

Delbin's steps faltered as they trudged toward the Tilt-A-Whirl. This part of the fair, full of light and laughter, usually cheered him, but his every glance seemed to land on something dark. Trash bins that needed to be changed. A child crying because she didn't win a toy. A half-eaten ice cream cone upended in the dirt. Gods of Moranaia, he would grow truly maudlin at this rate.

They neared the Tilt-A-Whirl, and he winced as a woman's cry sounded from the ride. Inona went tense, her hand slipping into her pocket as though she was reaching for her knife. Delbin lowered his palm to her shoulder and shook his head at her questioning glance.

"That was a scream of enjoyment, not danger."

"Who can tell?" Inona muttered. But she took her hand from her pocket and relaxed.

Delbin bypassed the short, crowded set of steps to the ride's entrance and headed for the small operator's station attached to the side. He waited until Tommy stopped the ride and started helping people to the exit before climbing over the rails and dropping behind the control panel with a flourish. Delbin peeked over at Inona, both her brows lifted at his antics.

"Couldn't you have used the stairs?"

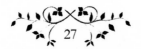

Some of his ill humor faded as he smirked. "Faster this way."

Inona leaned a shoulder against the pink side panel and gestured at the booth. "There's not room for me up there. What am I supposed to do?"

Before he could answer, Tommy returned. "All clear. I'm headed to the big wheel now. Trainin' someone new?"

"Nah. Just a friend." Though if she wanted more... No. Delbin cut that wish off and darted around Tommy before the line of guests grew too impatient. "Catch you later."

Tommy leered as he climbed down the side next to Inona but didn't have time to flirt. If they were short-handed, Grunge would be antsy. No use holding things up any longer than necessary. Delbin opened the entrance gate, taking tickets and directing the guests toward the cars. He only had to ask two children to stand by the measuring stick—both kids were tall enough, fortunately—before he could do the safety check and return to the controls.

"All right, folks, keep both hands on the rails while the ride is moving," he announced into the microphone above the control panel. "Remain seated at all times, and do not attempt to leave the car until the ride has come to a complete stop."

Delbin hit the start button. *And for the love of the Divine, please don't puke.*

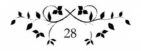

By the time night had fallen, Inona had shifted from doubt about Delbin to certainty—something was not right with him. He *worked,* and it was clear he was used to it. He operated the ride with a casual ease that could only be borne of experience. When one of the spinning cars started sticking, he climbed in to fix it. He smiled and chatted with the guests. He'd even cleaned up after a sick child without complaint.

If he'd decided to contribute to society, why wouldn't he have petitioned to return to Moranaia?

Smiling in reassurance, she directed the next child in line to stand by the height line. Inona couldn't fit up top with Delbin, so he'd given her this task. It wasn't too bad. Except… "I'm sorry. You're not quite tall enough."

The little girl's lip stuck out. "I'm seven. I'm big enough!"

"Well, you don't want to be flung out of the ride, do you?" Inona asked. Quite reasonably, she thought. "I don't think you could be healed from that type of disaster."

"Flung out?"

A choked cough sounded behind her, and Inona looked away from the suddenly pale child to Delbin. "What?" she asked.

She felt the brush of his mind against hers. But this time, her body heated in something decidedly not anger. She clamped down on her self-control and let his thoughts flow in. *"Don't terrify the humans, Inona."*

Humor seeped into his every word. She shot him a frustrated glance. *"Shouldn't she know the risk?"*

"Perhaps not so…vividly."

As he coughed again, a sorry attempt to stifle a laugh, Inona cut off the connection. The girl still stood, biting her

lip as she stared at the ride. Inona sighed. Maybe that *had* been a bit much. "I'm sorry," she said, catching the child's attention. "I was just teasing."

"My sister's on there," the girl whispered. "She's tall. I think."

Clechtan. Inona knelt down to meet the child's eyes. "She'll be fine. The only person who's actually been flung off of the ride is Delbin up there, and he seems okay."

The girl's mouth fell open, and her gaze shot to Delbin. Then she laughed. "You're really joking?"

The humans wouldn't ride these things if they weren't safe, right? Inona gave a decisive nod. "Absolutely. But you really do have to be as tall as the line to get on."

"Cass!" a woman called from a nearby bench. "I told you they wouldn't let you on. Come wait for your sister."

The little girl danced away, waving, her faith in the ride restored. As the whirling began again, Inona darted a glance over her shoulder. If only her faith in the metal contraption was so strong. But Delbin didn't seem the type to lead people to their doom. As the night progressed, she became more certain of it. He was not what he seemed.

Finally, another fair worker arrived to relieve them. As Delbin climbed down, he glanced back at Stephie. "How's Meggie's girl?"

"A bit better," the woman answered. "Shouldn't need a doctor, thank God."

Delbin nodded and grasped Inona's hand. "Good. She's been saving too long for her own trailer for that kind of hit." He waved. "See you later!"

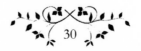

They walked in silence for a few moments, but Inona couldn't hold in her curiosity for long. "What did you mean, 'that kind of hit'?"

"Healers are not a given here," Delbin said. "Human healthcare is different."

Her hand tightened around his. "And you stay here?" she blurted.

His lips twisted. "I don't have a choice."

"No one is banned forever. Not if they'll abide by our laws." Anger coursed through her as she gestured at the Tilt-A-Whirl. "You obviously don't mind work. With your magical talent, you could do many things on Moranaia. Don't tell me you don't have a choice."

"It's not..." His voice trailed off, and his eyes went wide. "Do you feel that?"

Her stomach lurched as the world pulsed sickly around her for several unending heartbeats. Then it was gone. Around them, the humans carried on, no sign of distress on their faces. Her eyes met Delbin's. "What...?"

"Something happened to the energy here." His mouth turned down. "But I can't tell what."

She tugged at his hand. "Let's go find out."

Delbin hurried into his tent and grabbed his backpack. Even after a hundred uneventful years on Earth, he kept an emergency pack prepared. Humans in this country didn't tend to believe in the supernatural, and people, here at least, didn't fear being burned at the stake. Yet that didn't mean

there was no danger, as humans also tended to capture or kill what they didn't understand. He had to be ready to move quickly if he was discovered.

After slinging the backpack over his shoulder, Delbin paused. His eyes slipped closed as he followed the trail of odd energy through the web of magic that connected all life. A discordant note, a hint of wrongness…. There. He frowned as he tried to pinpoint the location. It wasn't the portal, a point he could detect easily. They'd have to drive out in search of the origin.

Delbin ducked out of the tent and met Inona's gaze. "Best I can tell, it's coming from somewhere to the north. Maybe the state park."

Inona gave a quick glance around before answering in a low voice. "We have to find it."

With a nod, Delbin headed for the truck. His every instinct told him to pull power into himself to prepare for conflict, but the energy pulsed in odd ways. He'd been more and more hesitant of doing too much magic in some locations, as some areas left him feeling ill if he tried to connect to the energy. Now, it shifted back and forth between that sickly feel and something closer to normal.

Maybe his earlier confrontation with Kien hadn't been a coincidence.

He rounded the front of the truck as Inona climbed into the passenger seat, but he stopped short at the sight of Grunge stepping out of the shadows. "I know we're short-handed, but I need to—"

"Go and figure out this mess," Grunge said, nodding.

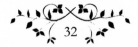

Peering into Grunge's face, Delbin caught the slightest flicker of power. A few breaths of time where he could see a younger face beneath the glamour. "You've noticed the change in energy, too? Why didn't you say anything?"

"Didn't want to," he answered with a shrug. "Now go fix it. I'll find someone to fill in if you're not back in time for the morning shift."

Delbin gave a quick salute. "Thanks, Grunge."

As the Sidhe walked away, Delbin hopped into the truck and snapped on his seat belt. At least he wouldn't have to worry about losing his job. With a smile, he started the ignition and threw the truck into gear.

He glanced at Inona to see if his silence bothered her and frowned to see her pallor. "Sorry."

"Why?" He saw her study him out of the corner of his eye. "I'm not upset," she said.

"You're pale."

She surprised him by laughing. "We're hurtling over the ground in a metal contraption. I've been in human transports before, but… How can you do this so often? I don't know how anyone gets used to this."

"Your job is to cross through the Veil between worlds, but a truck makes you nervous?" It was his turn to chuckle. Magic might make life easy, but that ease often stifled innovation. "These things move fast, but they won't get you lost for centuries."

Her chin lifted. "I've never been lost in the Veil."

"Wow." One side of Delbin's mouth curved up. "Not even during training? Impressive."

"I had a good teacher," Inona said primly, though he could hear the humor in her tone.

"Still, the Veil's tricky," he argued.

"Well…" Inona paused as he took a sharp right and then turned left onto a narrow, curvy mountain road. When she spoke again, her voice was tenser than before. "Kai *did* have to come after me once, but I wouldn't say I was lost. Misplaced a little, maybe. All strands lead somewhere."

Delbin gave her a sidelong glance. "I wouldn't have pegged you as an optimist."

"I'm not." He caught her shrug. "But I'm not a pessimist, either. Life is never one way or the other."

He considered her words as he turned onto another, less populated road. *Never one way or the other.* Delbin supposed she was right. Ups and downs traded places like cars on a Ferris wheel. He was example enough of that. He might've had to leave his home, but he'd been content on Earth, sometimes even happy. In the last few years, he'd found good friends among the hard-working carnival folk. Many of his earlier jobs had been equally rewarding.

But not all.

"We aren't too far from the portal now," Inona said.

Delbin pushed his ruminations aside to focus on the area. The roads wound around and between the forested mountains, neighborhoods and shopping centers appearing where they could. If the trees were more ancient and the buildings better blended into the environment, the place wouldn't be too far off from Moranaia.

Chattanooga was definitely one of his favorite stops on the east coast route.

The trees thinned, and he caught sight of a neighborhood in the distance. "Annoying that they've built so close to the portal."

"I hope it doesn't cause a problem," she answered, gaze focused ahead. "There was no sign of discovery at the portal, but we'll need to heighten shielding. Or seal this particular gate. Most humans aren't connected to the flow of magic well enough to slip into the Veil's energy, but you never know. It's going to take careful watching."

"Better you than me."

She snorted. "Thanks."

Delbin drove past the portal's location and continued beyond the houses. The trail of dark energy was farther north. "This is across the river from the official state park, but the mountains here are fairly tall. Let's head up the mountain. There are lots of places to hide up there. Caves and such."

For a moment, she didn't answer. "Why are you helping with this? You don't care about Moranaia or—"

"I do care about Moranaia," he retorted. His hands tightened on the steering wheel. "Or I would have stayed."

More silence. Then hesitantly she spoke. "Tell me."

Should he? Coric knew most of the truth and had kept his confidence, but Delbin hadn't told him for a decade after being exiled. What if Inona wasn't trustworthy? He eyed her as best he could in the dark truck cab and caught her earnest expression before his focus returned to the road. Was there even a point in his silence anymore?

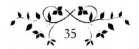

"You said there was no note in my records of my brother, but it was for my brother that I left," Delbin finally said.

He sensed her gaze on his face like a caress. "Wait. You left voluntarily?"

"Lord Moren helped me. Kai's brother?"

"That's right. You were from Oria," she said. "Why would you do such a thing. Why would he?"

Delbin speared her with a quick, intense glance. "You can tell no one, Inona."

"I can't promise that," she said, her voice rising. "I will not betray Lord Lyr."

"It is not a betrayal. Coric knows, and he's one of the most loyal people I've ever met." Delbin gripped the wheel tighter. She hadn't promised, but the story spilled out. "My brother was an infant when my powers fully manifested. My telepathy is powerful, Inona. Powerful enough to insert my thoughts into others' minds with ease. When that became apparent, my mother spoke with Lord Moren about sending me away."

"Your mother?" Inona asked. "How old were you?"

"Sixteen."

Her shocked cry echoed in the quiet cab. "You were a *child?* That was not in the report on you. I don't understand."

"A child by elven standards, but old enough to manage on Earth. At least a century ago." Delbin ran a hand through his hair. "Allafon is…dangerous. He's never committed treason, but he is not kind to his retainers. There was a real threat in him finding out about me. My mother and brother might very well have become his guests and me his puppet. I had to disappear."

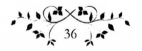

"My Gods," she whispered as he turned down the road leading to the trailhead he sought. "Delbin...Allafon is dead."

He slammed his foot on the brakes, jostling them both against the seat belts as the truck jerked. "Dead?"

Inona tossed an uneasy look out the back window. "Move out of the road."

Delbin forced himself to resume driving even as his heart slammed hard in his chest. "How long has he been dead?"

"A good month or two now."

He sucked in a pained breath and directed the truck into a dark, empty parking lot. In silence, he jerked the gear stick to park. "And Moren hasn't come for me."

"I suppose not."

He felt Inona's eyes on his face once more, but he didn't look at her. Couldn't. "I can't believe this. And no mention of my brother?"

"Moren has been busy," she said softly. "Allafon might not have committed treason when you were there, but he found his way to it eventually. He tried to murder Kai, Lyr, and Lyr's newfound daughter. Kai killed him as he began a blood magic spell. As Allafon's heir, Moren had a great deal to handle after that."

Delbin stared out the window at the shadowed trees. "Perhaps he killed my brother after all. He was excellent at finding reasons to hurt others. All these years..."

Inona unbuckled her seatbelt and slid closer. "I don't know. But the time wasn't wasted. There's no telling what he might have done with access to your power. Having someone

able to take over minds under his control… There's a real chance he would have succeeded in his plans."

"I suppose." Delbin swallowed hard, fighting the urge to lean closer to her. "With Allafon dead, I guess it doesn't matter who you tell now."

She settled her hand on his shoulder. "Why didn't your mother go to Lyr's father Telien? He was a fair leader."

"Tyrants are clever, Inona." Delbin let out a long breath and gave in, relaxing a little beneath the weight of her hand. "It's difficult to explain the mantle of fear he'd placed on us. Nothing he did was overtly illegal, after all, and he was careful with the 'accidents' that befell those who opposed him. It was never his fault. Lord Moren did his best to mediate. We all believed it safer if he exiled me."

Her eyes narrowed on his face. "Sixteen is too young to be exiled as a shirker. You'd still be an apprentice even now."

"Age is just a number, so they say." Delbin's lips tilted up. "Literally, in my case. Easy enough for Moren to alter the records."

"I can't believe Lyr didn't have Moren's head for this," Inona muttered.

Delbin lifted his hand to cover hers as she gave his shoulder a squeeze. "Maybe he doesn't know."

"Moren is lord of Oria now. Surely—"

"As you said, there's much for him to deal with," Delbin said. "Once we've found out what Kien is up to, maybe I'll go back with you. Find out what happened to my brother."

Have a few choice words with Moren.

The energy pulsed around them again, but Delbin held her gaze. Finally, she nodded. "Let's go, then."

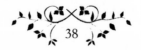

4

Inona stared at Delbin's back as they hiked down the deserted trail. Her elven eyesight was keen enough to avoid disaster, but she nonetheless stayed close enough to reach out and touch him. And *not* just because she wanted to touch him. How had he managed in the human world at such a young age? It was phenomenal. *He* was phenomenal.

Odd energy tingled along her skin as they grew nearer to the source of the disturbance. With a shudder, Inona sent her mind toward Delbin's and brushed against the edge of his thoughts.

He connected immediately. *"We can't just rush in,"* she sent. *"We should've come up with a plan."*

"It's simple. You'll hide while I go in. Then you save me if I don't come out."

Inona's steps slowed in surprise, but she forced herself forward. *"I am a trained* sonal. *I'm not going to hide while you go into danger."*

Delbin smirked over his shoulder. *"I'm not questioning your fierceness. Rawr."* His eyes twinkled with suppressed laughter before he faced forward again. *"But Kien saw you earlier. How am I supposed to find out what's going on if you're with me?"*

"No." Her skin chilled at the very thought of him going in alone. *"You aren't here to confront him. We're doing as much scouting as we can without being caught, and then we're heading back to Moranaia to report."*

He was quiet for so long she wasn't certain he was going to answer. *"But we could find out a lot if I pretend to join him."*

"I said no. And I have seniority." Inona reached out and poked him with her finger, but he only smirked at her again. She sighed. *"Think. Allafon might have used you for your talents. What if Kien's goal is the same? He must have chosen to approach you for* some *reason."*

That erased Delbin's smug look. *"Good point."*

"We're getting close, I think." Inona tugged at his wrist until he stopped. *"We need to switch places. I'm trained to navigate the forest without a trail, so I'll do better in the lead. You cast about us for signs of life. Unless scouting is another skill of yours?"*

He gestured at the woods. *"Lead away, my lady."*

Inona rolled her eyes at him as she passed, but she couldn't hold back a smile. His good humor was contagious. But he'd had opportunity enough to cultivate it, considering all he'd been through from such a young age. Sixteen. She shook her head as she ducked between the trees. Criminally young.

The moonlight barely trickled through the thick trees overhead, but it was enough. Inona led them steadily through the underbrush, heading ever closer to the source of the

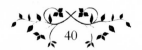

pulsing magic. Each throb was more erratic than the last, a heart struggling to control its blood. It was far from normal. Earth in particular had steady, reliable magic, if much less than that of Moranaia and most of the fae dimensions.

This fractured energy was no coincidence.

Inona stopped abruptly at the sight of a small clearing that ended in the wall of a short ridge. Flickering light caught her eye, and she peered at the stone wall. A slit about half again her height glowed softly—an entrance. Although caves were common in this area, the sickly energy emanating from the opening was not. She crouched low and gestured for Delbin to duck behind a tree. Carefully, she scanned the area. No people in sight.

"Do you sense anything?" she sent to Delbin. Telepaths were among the best at detecting others, since thoughts were tied so closely to the energy of life.

"There are three inside," he answered immediately. *"Poor shielding on two of them. They're arguing."*

Inona squinted at the small entrance. The glow was faint, and from the positioning, she was fairly certain that a long tunnel curved away from the opening. Otherwise, they'd be able to see the people within. What should they do? If something was damaging the very energy of Earth, Lord Lyr would want to know of it at once.

"Can you tell their distance?"

A pause, and then Delbin answered. *"Several feet to the left and deeper back. I think."*

Inona scrunched her brows, considering. *"We should stay and watch. See if they leave."*

"They aren't going to leave," Delbin answered. *"One of them is trying to hold together some kind of spell. The other two are arguing about what they're going to do about Kien."*

"What do you mean?"

"He left a few days ago after something happened to the spell." Delbin shifted closer until his shoulder brushed hers. Then he let out a soft curse. *"We need to stop them. Now. They're poisoning Earth's energy field. That's why it has felt off. If they gain control of that spell again, they'll stand a better chance of succeeding."*

"The mage has been holding this together for days?" She bit her lip. *"That doesn't make sense. Really, I don't see how they could affect the entire Earth from here."*

Delbin fell silent for a moment before connecting with her again. *"Sorry. I delved deeper. They placed nodes all over the place, all connected. A different node was destroyed, but all that energy had to go somewhere. It backlashed along the connection. Now this one is about to blow, too."*

Her breath caught. *"Why would they do that? Energy is life."*

"Domination," Delbin answered immediately. *"Get rid of other magic users with the poison and then unleash your own powers on the unsuspecting humans. There'd be no one left to stop you."*

Clechtan. Did Lord Lyr know about this? If Delbin was correct, they didn't have time to find out. Inona scanned the clearing, expanding her senses in a sweep. She didn't detect anyone outside the cave. But then, the assassins sent after Lyr had been able to slip through shielding.

"Any idea if there are more?" she asked.

In the light of the moon spilling through the thinning trees, she watched as his eyes lost focus. After a moment,

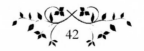

he shook his head and fixed his attention on her face once more. *"None in their thoughts. But I planted an idea. When one of them comes out, let him take me."*

Inona scowled. *"Didn't we discuss this?"*

"In sight of them, I can take control of their minds."

"What?" Her mouth fell open, and she forced it shut with a snap. *"I've heard of Prince Ralan doing such a thing. And a few others. But you're not formally trained. How can you be certain?"*

A hard, sad glint entered his eyes. *"You learn much as a teenager in a strange world, Inona."*

An ache settled in her chest at the hint of pain pinching his face. What had he been forced to do? Earth wasn't a terrible place, but it wasn't necessarily safe, either, especially for those who were different. Laws varied so wildly, and exiles had to not only hide their true natures but recreate their lives on a regular basis.

She'd believed only the worst of their people ended up in such a situation. She'd even wondered about her own prince after he'd chosen to live on Earth. How many exiles were not what they seemed? For the first time, she found herself wanting to know their stories more than how strictly they followed the rules.

"Something needs to be done," Inona said. *"There could be others who—"*

"He's coming out now," Delbin interrupted. *"I'll try to get in and out quickly. If things go wrong, you can rescue me."*

"But—"

Delbin cut off their link and ducked around the tree as a red-haired man stepped out of the cave. "Ah, I've found

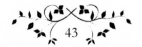

you," Delbin called in a jovial tone, and the man froze, his hand shifting to a weapon at his side. "Prince Kien said there would be friends here."

The man's expression went slack, and his hands dropped to his sides. Without a word, he led Delbin into the cave. Just like that, they were gone.

This wasn't going to be as easy as Delbin had led Inona to believe. He had taken control of minds before, but only for a brief time when under duress. In his early days on Earth, he'd used his magic to defend himself, but quick mental blasts or suggestions were more effective than control. He'd only done it a handful of times.

He was almost certainly going to be captured within minutes of entering. But a few moments were all he needed. If he could coerce the person holding the spell to release it, the spell would break. From what Delbin had read in their minds, they wouldn't be able to recreate it quickly.

Delbin followed the one named Patrick through the growing golden light of the tunnel. It was longer than he'd thought. Had his mental range grown? It hadn't been so easy to find others' minds when he was younger. His time in the dunk tank must have given him steady practice. But his heartbeat still pounded in his ears as they entered a large cavern. Stalagmites and stalactites speared like teeth around them, water pooling like saliva in puddles on the floor.

His nose crinkled at that mental image. Yeah, no.

In the center, one of the men stood in front of a column of rock. His body blocked sight of the spell's focal point, and he didn't turn when the third let out an exclamation and rushed forward. "What are you doing, Patrick?"

"Kien invited him," Patrick answered, his voice a little hollow under Delbin's control.

As the man eyed him uncertainly, Delbin took a deep breath. Then with a quick jab of power, he forced his mind past the other's shielding and tried to assert control. This one fought against him, trying to shove him away so forcefully that Delbin's head began to ache. By the time he finally succeeded, sweat beaded his brow and dampened his palms.

Unlike Patrick, this one—Victor—was difficult to contain. Wiping his memory would be a much harder task.

The only sounds in the cavern now were the steady drips of water sliding from countless stalactites and the harsh, panting breaths of the third man. Despite his companions' sudden silence, he hadn't moved. Delbin frowned. Would controlling his mind be the best way to distract him? He was already trembling with the effort of holding the other two, and this one was stronger. But the guy hadn't twitched a muscle even when his companions went silent. Controlling the spell?

Delbin crept around the edge of the cavern as he angled for a better view. His gaze narrowed on a glint of light in the middle of the column. *No, not a column.* In the spot where a stalagmite and stalactite almost joined, a crystal the size of a child's fist hovered. Eyes closed, the third man held his hands around it as it pulsed with a murky, gray light.

Tentatively, Delbin extended his power, searching for the extent of the mage's shielding. Almost at once, he drew back. Yeah, that wasn't going to be easy to crack, and he would lose control of the other two in the attempt. But the mage seemed so intent on holding the spell together that he wasn't paying attention to the rest of the room.

If Delbin had learned anything, it was that magic didn't solve everything.

He glanced around the cavern floor until he found a piece of some hapless stalagmite that had broken. He bent down and grasped it. Then he paused again as Patrick shifted, fighting against Delbin's control. *Better speed this up.* He grasped the worn hunk of minerals, drew back his arm, and let it fly.

It hit squarely against the mage's left wrist, shoving his hand against the pulsing crystal. The man's eyes snapped open, and he screamed as the sickly light flared brightly. Delbin ducked behind a wide stone column, releasing his mental hold on the others to reinforce his own shielding. He barely had time to wipe Patrick's memory before all hell broke loose.

"Which one of you fools did that?" the mage shouted against a growing hum emanating from the crystal. "What have you done?"

"There was another one," Victor answered.

"What other one?"

Delbin didn't even try to follow the argument. Couldn't they feel the danger? He shoved his hands against his ears as pressure began to build, but it was more magical than physical. Then the light exploded, filling the cavern until

Delbin had to close his eyes against it. A sharp crack sounded, loud enough to hear despite his covered ears.

The mage yelled a curse, but any further words were drowned by a loud crackle and one final, grinding snap. As the light cut off abruptly, the ground began to shake. Delbin's arms shifted to cover his head as bits of stalactites rained down. But the energy that had released from the crystal was beautiful. Healthy.

Moranaian.

"So help me, Patrick—"

"I didn't do anything," Patrick interrupted. "I was just standing here."

"Where'd your new friend go, then?" Victor asked.

"I don't know what you're talking about."

"Dammit, this was the last node standing after the Moranaians used their counter spell. We're going to have to redo the whole thing. Years wasted because—"

"Silence!"

As another voice rang through the dark cavern, Delbin flinched and scrambled to reinforce his mental shielding. *Kien.* He forced his breaths to slow, though panic gnawed at his insides. Had the prince found Inona on his way in? He sent out a quick mental search and slumped in relief to find her alive and well.

But Delbin probably wouldn't fare so well. Trapped in a cavern with the dark prince and his minions?

Yeah, he was screwed.

5

Rough bark bit into Inona's back as she pressed herself hard against the tree. She'd almost been caught. She wasn't certain why she *hadn't* been caught. Kien had appeared out of nowhere, his steps silent even though he moved with the slow, shuffling gait of the recently injured. But he'd barely glanced around the forest before he'd stumbled into the narrow cave opening.

What was she going to do? She was *not* going to leave Delbin in there alone.

Suddenly, the energy around her gave an odd lurch, shifting like a wayward strand in the Veil. For one long moment, the ground trembled. Inona covered her head and hoped that the earthquakes here weren't like the ones on the plains back home. Those were sometimes fierce enough to level cities, at least near fault lines.

Thankfully, this tremor was over in moments. Inona peered around her tree at the cave once the earth had calmed. No movement. Gods, she hoped Delbin hadn't been injured. Had Kien unleashed some dark magic? She sent her senses out, and she gasped to find...Moranaian energy? The sick oddness was gone.

At the edge of her consciousness, she detected Delbin's presence. Just a quick brush, probably to see if she was well, but Inona latched on before he drew away. *"What happened? Did they catch you?"*

"No." There was a long pause, and she could feel his worry like her own. *"I disrupted what the mage was doing, and the spell just kind of exploded. Now Kien's here."*

"Can you get out?"

"I don't know. I'm barely hiding myself." Their connection wavered. *"I'm going to try something. I'll let you know."*

Just like that, the mental link was gone. Inona glared at the cave as though Delbin could actually see her. He'd been too long on his own if he could dismiss her orders so easily. By all the gods of Arneen, he wasn't even formally trained. What was he thinking? Scowling, she slipped a knife from her pocket and sneaked to the next tree. Then the next.

Chances were good she was going to have to save him.

Delbin's heart pounded as he sent his mind ever so slowly back into Patrick's, the youngest and weakest of the bunch. But he didn't try to assert control. What he really needed was to see, so he eased himself into a connection just strong enough to get hazy images of what was going on. The stalagmite hid him from sight, but it also blocked

his view. No way he wanted to move around and risk being seen.

"What have you idiots done?" Kien yelled, his voice an odd echo through both Patrick's and Delbin's ears.

Victor took a tentative step forward. "Wasn't me. Pat here brought some newcomer. I think. I blanked out until after the spell exploded."

Delbin felt Patrick's fear like his own as Kien turned his attention on him. "You brought a stranger here?"

"I don't know what he's talking about," Patrick forced out.

"There has to be some reason that Tom is unconscious and the spell ruined," Kien said, his tone smooth but his eyes spitting fury. "I don't suppose you have an explanation?"

"Milord, I swear—"

"Oh, shut up." Kien's expression went hard. "Describe this stranger, Victor."

Victor shifted uncertainly at the prince's attention. "It was a man. Had short blond hair. Patrick said you invited him. Then everything went dark."

Delbin bit back a curse. Too bad he hadn't been able to erase Victor's memory. Through Patrick, he watched a considering glint enter Kien's eyes before his lips lifted into a wicked smile. That couldn't be good.

"I see." Kien tapped a finger against his chin. "I did invite a young mind mage I stumbled upon, but perhaps he did not arrive with good intent. Patrick, check on Tom. Victor, you search the cavern."

Yep. Screwed.

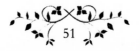

Releasing Patrick's mind once more, Delbin scanned the edges of the cavern for some way out. His eyes narrowed. Was that a tunnel between those two stalagmites a few feet away? The caves here branched out and connected all over the place, but it was risky to navigate them without experience or equipment. Was the possibility of death-by-cave better than whatever Kien might dish out?

Based on the look of dark fury on the prince's face, definitely better.

He just had to hustle before Victor made it to Delbin's area of the cavern. Giving a quick glance to either side, Delbin slipped to the next stalagmite. Then a spiraling column. He winced as his foot slid into a shallow pool, but there was nothing he could do about the water that leaked into his boot. At least it hadn't made a splash.

Delbin stepped onto a broad stone ledge near the mouth of the small tunnel and ducked between a pair of fang-like stalactites. As the damp sole of his shoe lost traction against the rock, he stifled a cry. Slipping, he threw out his hand for balance and connected with one of the stalactites.

He let out a relieved breath as he regained his footing. But then the fragile rock broke under his weight. Pieces tumbled down, splashing into another shallow pool, and he heard a shout. Dammit. He crouched low, trying to dart into the tunnel before he was seen, but a hand wrapped around his arm, jerking him to a stop.

"Gotcha!"

Gathering power from the world around him, Delbin let himself be spun around. A mental blast would incapacitate

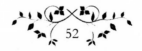

the man, and Delbin might be able to use the distraction to escape. Energy pooled in his body, like a buzzing in the blood. He looked into Victor's eyes and prepared to release it.

Then a shock slammed into Delbin like lightning, and his power drained away with every pain-filled heartbeat. He reached for his head. A vain attempt to stem the agony. His vision shifted to red.

Then black.

Now that the energy was cleaner, Inona pulled power into herself with abandon as she crept down the tunnel. She might not be a mage, but like most *sonal*, she could cloak herself from sight at least somewhat. Too bad she couldn't blast Kien with a battle spell. She'd just have to rely on stealth and her knife.

It was dim in the tunnel, but her eyes adjusted quickly to the shifting light. Gods, she hated caves. Why couldn't Kien have set his base in the trees? She would far rather climb than slink around rock formations with a mountain above her head.

The light grew brighter, so Inona cast a camouflaging spell around herself. It wouldn't make her invisible, but it helped distract the eye. She just had to keep her movements steady and slow. Way slower than she wanted after hearing Delbin cry out. But she'd been in enough difficult situations to know that rushing would help nothing.

A voice echoed from the cavern ahead. "Tie him up."

"You aren't going to kill him?" another said.

"Do not question me," the first man answered in a cold, regal voice. Probably Kien.

The sound of shuffling grew louder as she neared, and then the snap of something breaking rang out. Inona's heart gave a leap, but it settled at the tinkling of stone tumbling on stone. One of the men cursed.

"Stalagmites aren't going to hold him up," a voice said. "Must be made of flowstone. Damn things keep breaking."

"Maybe if you weren't trying to tie near the top—"

"Shut up!" Kien's shout reverberated down the tunnel. "No need to string him up. Just tie his hands together and bring him over."

"Don't you want to torture him?"

A pause. "Perhaps later."

Inona crouched low behind a large rock formation and peeked around the edge. A few body-lengths away, Kien stood glaring, his profile outlined in the dim glow of the mage lights dangling overhead. *Clechtan,* she cursed to herself. She edged back slowly so the movement wouldn't catch his eye. She would have to work her way over to the huge stalagmite to her right. That would be a perfect spot to ambush him.

A groan filled the cavern. "He's waking up," one of the voices said.

"Then work faster," Kien snarled.

Though her instinct was to check on Delbin, Inona used the distraction to creep to a better position. Once behind the stalagmite, she glanced around the edge at Kien's back. He

hadn't noticed her, best she could tell, his attention focused on the two men tying Delbin's hands behind his back.

A muffled sound from the side caught her attention. Inona's gaze narrowed on another man slumped against a column. Another prisoner? But he wasn't bound in any way, and his expression was detached as he watched the two tying Delbin. He did appear ill, his skin a sickly, pale yellow in the dim light.

"Blast him again," the third man mumbled.

"No," Kien said, his tone hard with command. "I have questions for him. Let him wake."

Inona moved shifted closer, this time behind a stalagmite near enough to Kien that she could almost touch him. But she didn't move against him. Instead, she focused on Delbin and waited along with the others as he returned to awareness.

He groaned again and shook his head. Then his body stiffened, and he started to tug against his bonds. "The hell?"

"Delbin," Inona whispered into his mind. *"Kien's men caught you. I'm in here."*

He stilled. *"Run. Warn Moranaia of his plans."*

"You're mistaken if you think I'm the type to leave a person to torture," she answered. *"Cause a distraction. Keep their attention. That's all I need."*

"I do hope you're ready to tell me your name now," Kien said. "Perhaps you will find yourself a little more forthcoming, hmm?"

"Fuck that," Delbin said.

Then he rolled to the left, shoving hard against the legs of one of his captors. The man tumbled over with a yelp, and his body slammed into the second man as he fell.

Inona didn't wait to see what else might happen. She tightened her hand around the hilt of her blade and slipped behind Kien. She took a deep, bracing breath for only a heartbeat, then struck.

Thank the gods she was tall.

Inona flung her left arm around his waist and wrapped her right over his shoulder, pressing her knife to his throat. His body jerked, and her brows rose at the hissing groan of pain he released as her left arm tightened. She could feel, then, the extra fabric around his waist where he'd been bandaged. He really had been injured recently.

Her gaze flicked to Delbin, and she winced to see him pinned against the rocky ground. One of his captors had his knee in Delbin's back. The other stood above them, a blade clutched in his hand.

"Call them off," she said into Kien's ear as she let the knife cut into his skin ever so slightly.

Enough to release blood. Enough for the steel blade to affect his magic.

"I should have known," Kien bit out through gritted teeth. "You're not Moranaian at all, are you? No scout there would carry steel. What game is this?"

A smile he couldn't see crossed her lips. "Wouldn't you like to know? Now call them off."

"Leave him be!" Kien called.

The second man stepped back at once. The one holding Delbin scowled for a moment, then shoved himself away. Delbin grunted as the man pushed him none too gently into the rock on his way up.

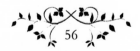

"Help him up," Inona ordered.

The men glared at her, but at Kien's nod, one of them leaned down and heaved Delbin to his feet. The man shoved him forward. Delbin stumbled and almost fell again before righting himself.

From the side, a chuckle rang out. The third man. Inona frowned as she studied his face. She should have considered this plan more thoroughly. He'd appeared sick, but what if she'd been wrong?

"Guess you're not as powerful as you seem," the man choked out around his laughter.

Kien went rigid, and she could practically feel the rage emanating from him. "Says the man who let our entire plan fail. If you've power that wasn't drained, shut up and act."

The laughter ceased, leaving a deep silence. The two behind Delbin exchanged uneasy glances and then turned their doubt-filled gazes on Kien. Were they less loyal than she'd assumed? But then one of them spoke.

"What should we do?"

"Unbind my friend," Inona answered, putting force behind her words. "Or I'll slice Kien's throat."

Kien chuckled. "You wouldn't."

Inona dug the knife a little deeper, and he let out an involuntary cry. "I am more than ready to dispense with any threat."

Power hummed around her as her captive tried to draw energy to himself despite the steel. Inona shoved her arm hard into his injured side, and he gasped, his magic sputtering out. "Untie him," Kien ground out.

What was she going to do with the prince? As the other two untied Delbin, she considered the dilemma. She couldn't let Kien go. He was a serious threat to Moranaia, and if she couldn't take him to Lord Lyr without getting Delbin killed, then she might have to kill Kien herself. It wasn't ideal. The dark magic was troublesome, and she had no way of knowing what other plans he might have.

But how could she take him alive? By all accounts, Kien was a powerful mage. An illusionist. The slightest slip and he'd turn on her. *Miaran*, but she hadn't been prepared for this. Who would have expected to find their greatest enemy on such a simple mission? Apparently, she should have.

Delbin rubbed at his wrists once the rope fell away. He turned his gaze on one of the men beside him. "Thanks, Patrick."

Patrick's eyes glazed over, his body slightly slack. Had Delbin taken control? Kien straightened, restless against her hold. "Do not think to try for my mind, youngling."

"Yeah, I don't want to see the messed up stuff in there. Thanks anyway," Delbin answered. Then he shifted his attention to the other man. "How about you help my friend? You have some rope ready, see? Go tie up Kien."

"I will torture you for days," Kien growled.

Inona shoved against his wound again to cut off his words. Though her arm grew damp with his blood, she didn't waver.

"Don't forget the third one," Inona said as she met Delbin's eyes.

The man against the column laughed. "Take the fool. I'm done with this shit."

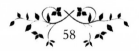

"You'll rule nothing without my help," Kien said.

"It's not like we've been ruling anything with it."

As the one with the rope tugged at Kien's hand, the prince jerked back. Inona tightened her hold, her knife slicing a fresh line. He cried out, flinching, and in that moment of distraction, the other man bound his hands in front with the sharp, awkward motions of someone under mental control.

Across the cavern, Delbin stared, unblinking, his body trembling. His face had gone pale, his breathing shallow. The effort of such control must be immense. They had to end this soon.

Inona removed her right arm from Kien's throat, turning the knife and hitting him in the side of the head with the pommel. He sagged against her, and she let out a grunt at his sudden weight. But she was strong enough to handle it. As Delbin ordered Patrick forward to help, Inona adjusted the prince in her hold and backed toward the entrance.

"How long can you keep control of them?" she asked.

"Not long."

Inona eyed the third man slumped against the column. "What about him?"

"Can't right now," Delbin muttered.

She frowned. Couldn't what? Then she realized what he meant. If Delbin couldn't control the man's mind, they should tie him up, too. It would be the best choice. But Delbin was clearly shaking now, and from his sharp words, it was obvious he was about to lose his hold. They needed to hustle.

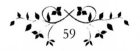

"They'll come after us as soon as you release them."

A grim smile crossed Delbin's pale face. "No. They won't."

Before she could ask what he meant, both men cried out, their hands going to their heads. Moments later they crumpled. Delbin sagged where he stood, and shadows like new bruises had formed beneath his eyes. But he didn't pause for long, stumbling across the cave to reach her.

With one last glance over her shoulder at the third man, Inona turned toward the exit. It was going to be difficult dragging Kien through the narrow space, but she didn't have much choice. Not unless Delbin had regained some strength.

"I know you're wiped out," she began.

"Here." Without further comment, he shifted to her side and slipped his shoulder under Kien's left arm. Together, they hefted the prince's weight and headed for the entrance. Now they just had to get him to the portal.

6

Every muscle in Delbin's body ached by the time they reached the truck. Hell, even his mental channels hurt. On top of the odd, electric blast that one bastard had used to knock him out, he'd drained himself heavily to take control of two minds two different times. Drawing in more energy had helped keep him upright and moving, but only sleep would cure the rest.

With a sigh, he stared at the truck. "So how are we doing this?"

"We'll put him in the back," Inona said.

Delbin eyed the half-full bed of the pickup. Pieces of broken carnival rides and a few storage bins filled most of the space, but there should be enough room for the prince. Still… "What if he wakes up?"

She winced. "Good question. Is there something we can tie him to? There's not room for me to sit beside him."

Letting her take the prince's weight, Delbin leaned over the edge of the truck bed and examined the thick metal rings in the side. Grunge had installed them so they could tie down equipment and tarps. Delbin grinned. *Bet he didn't expect them to be used to secure a prince.* Then again, there was no telling what the old Sidhe had seen over the years.

"We can bind him to the cargo rings," Delbin said. "They're steel like the truck bed. That should weaken him a lot."

"Good," Inona answered.

Delbin took Kien's shoulders while Inona lifted his feet. Together, they rolled the prince over the side of the truck where he landed with a thump and moan of pain. Delbin exchanged a worried glance with Inona.

"How long will he stay out?" he asked.

Inona peered over the side at the prince. "From a blow like that, probably not too much longer."

"That's what I was afraid of."

Delbin darted around her and tugged down the tailgate. With a smile for Inona, he leapt up and started searching through the toolbox at the back of the pile of junk. He shoved aside the ratchet straps and bungee cords. Great for securing non-living cargo, but not... Ah! Delbin snatched up the bundle of nylon rope. Then he edged his way around the prince's prone body until he reached his hands.

His attention on Kien's face, Delbin released a tendril of magic until his mind touched the edges of the prince's shields. Or what was left of them. In a few heartbeats, he'd eased through enough to confirm that Kien was hovering in that odd space between unconsciousness and awareness.

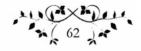

They couldn't let him wake up before reaching Moranaia.

Delbin hesitated. If he messed up his mental blast, it could wake Kien rather than the opposite. Damn. As he considered the problem, his fingers flew along the rope, the knot patterns habit after so long on the road. By the time he'd secured the prince to the metal rings on the side of the truck with the rope, he hadn't decided.

Then Kien groaned and twitched, and Delbin detected his mental shift toward wakefulness. No more time to debate. He gathered his power and sent it, like a dart, into the prince's mind.

"What's going on?" Inona whispered.

Delbin held up his hand, a silent signal for quiet. Had it worked? He searched the edges of the prince's mind. Only when he found blank unconsciousness could he let himself slump against the back of the cab in relief. And exhaustion. He rubbed against the ache in his temples. Then he straightened again and forced himself to move.

Quietly, Delbin crept back until he could jump out of the truck bed. Then he turned to Inona. "I had to put him under again."

She nodded. "Let's go."

They wasted no time hitting the road. Delbin had already backed out of the parking space by the time Inona had her seatbelt buckled, and with the hiking trails abandoned so late at night, he didn't feel bad about speeding through the dark parking lot and the road beyond. Good thing it wasn't daytime. No way they would've been able to get Kien tied in the back without being spotted.

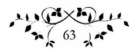

"I'm surprised he didn't camp closer to the portal," Inona said.

Delbin's gaze kept moving from the road to his rearview mirror, though he could barely make out the Kien-shaped lump in the back. "There was something about that column, I think."

He felt her stare. "What column?"

"Sorry. Forgot you weren't there for that," Delbin answered. "There was a place where a stalagmite and stalactite had almost formed a solid piece. In the gap, they'd placed a crystal. The focal point of the spell."

"I didn't see anything like that," she said. His gaze flicked to her at the worried tone of her voice. Her foot began to tap a restless beat as she continued. "We shouldn't have left the mage. We should have tied him up at least."

Delbin frowned at the dark road. "We didn't have a choice. Isn't Kien the priority?"

"Yes, of course." She sighed. "But I'm afraid not capturing those three is going to come back to haunt us."

Should he tell her what he'd done? Delbin had been exiled from Moranaia for so long he wasn't sure what the rules were for the situation. But there was only one way to find out. "I erased the memories of the two I'd been controlling. I didn't have the time or energy to wipe the mage, but I read him. He was serious about being done with Kien."

His nervousness built, twisting his insides, until Inona spoke. "This is going to be the strangest report I've ever given."

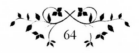

Delbin barked out a surprised laugh. "That's all you have to say about it?"

"You think I'm going to chide you?" Surprise laced her tone. "An exile isn't allowed to use magic for harm, generally speaking. But a situation like that was life or death. No one would expect you to choose death."

He considered her words as he followed the winding mountain road back toward the portal. Maybe he hadn't broken as many rules as he'd assumed when he'd first arrived here. The first ten years, he'd struggled the most, but he'd been careful not to wield his power for personal gain. He had learned the heady danger of using manipulation from Allafon's fine example.

Delbin refused to turn into the monster he could easily be.

As they turned down the road to the portal, Inona spoke. "Where are we going to stop? There's nowhere to park in the neighborhood, and it wouldn't be good to unload Kien in plain sight."

He snorted. "You've got that right. Never underestimate the ability of random people to do stupid stuff. Usually with no actual information about the matter."

"I can't tell if you're amused or bitter," Inona said. "Sounds like there's a story there."

"You move around as much as I do, you see more than enough examples of how people react." Delbin gave her a quick, wry smile before focusing on the road again. "And it's certainly not exclusive to humans."

Inona went silent for a moment.

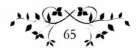

"So what do you suggest we do?" she finally asked.

He frowned. "Let me see if I can remember someplace close."

"Remember?"

"I make it a point to know the area around any portals on our route," Delbin answered. He passed the neighborhood, his gaze scanning the dark trees to his right. Yep, still there. He slowed and eased the truck onto a bumpy dirt driveway barely illuminated by the headlights. "There used to be an old house on the other side of the ridge from the portal. Not sure if anyone lives there, though."

Her voice rose over the rumbling sound of the truck. "What will happen if they do?"

"Nothing, probably. We'll stop before we get to the house."

The trees began to thin ahead, and the driveway curved toward the right. Moonlight poured across the empty expanse of hill rolling beyond. The far edge of that hill dropped away at the ridge, but it was impossible to see from this angle. He'd walked the area the last time the fair had visited Chattanooga, enjoying the energy of the portal. Dreaming of home. Hah. One hundred years of sacrifice might have been for nothing if his brother was dead.

Delbin's mouth tightened at the thought, but he only hit the brakes and shoved the vehicle into park. No use dwelling on a past that wouldn't change.

"Let's get going," he snapped, shoving himself out of the truck before Inona could comment.

Her door clicked shut as he crossed to the side, but she didn't speak. Fortunately. He couldn't explain his sudden

ill humor even to himself. Huffing out a breath, Delbin glanced over the side of the truck. Then he froze. The space where Kien had lain was empty, save a puddle of blood and a tangle of rope.

"Fuck," Delbin yelped.

Inona rushed over. "What?"

"He's gone."

She sank low, her gaze moving around the area as she pressed her back against the side of the truck. With a sharp tug on his wrist, Inona pulled him down beside her. "When did you last see him?"

Delbin thought back. Had he checked after turning down the dirt road? "On the main road for sure. When we turned under the trees, it was too dark."

"*Clechtan,*" she cursed. "We need to move. If he gets to the portal first, there's no telling where he'll go."

Before he could say a word, she darted out of sight.

Inona didn't bother waiting to see what Delbin would do. If Kien had escaped near the main road, he might have circled around the base of the ridge to the portal. Although it was technically spelled against letting him enter Moranaia, there were plenty of other realms he might escape to. Realms she wouldn't know to search.

Instead of heading directly across the open hill, Inona cut right until she reached the trees lining the south end of the ridge. She sent her senses out around her as far as she could with the minuscule energy available. No sign of Kien,

although she detected Delbin just behind her. As she ducked into the trees, she pulled her knives and worked her way carefully toward the portal.

They rounded the base of the hill, and the gentle slope gave way to the sharp line of the ridge wall. Inona gave Delbin a mental nudge. *"I don't sense him. You?"*

A brief pause. *"No. Dammit. I should've kept mental control, but it takes so much energy."*

"Which isn't exactly plentiful on Earth," she grumbled. Then a new thought hit her. *"Are you sure it was really him? That illusion he did this morning was quite realistic. I'm not sure of the extent of an illusionist's power."*

"Illusions don't bleed, or if they did, they wouldn't leave any blood behind. There was a pool of blood in the back of the truck."

At least that was one worry gone. But Inona hadn't sensed him by the time they approached the portal, and a quick examination of the area showed no signs of disturbance. No footprints, no blood. She closed her eyes and connected to the shields around the portal. Thankfully, no one had passed through.

Where could he have gone? Back to the cave? Maybe he had some way to detect them so he could stay out of sight.

"You said there's an old house on the north side of the ridge?" she asked.

"Yes." He frowned. *"Well, more northwest. You think he's there?"*

"I suppose we'll have to find out."

In silence, they followed the ridge until they reached the line of trees. The stone wall had shrunk to waist height, and

it wasn't long until the ridge disappeared into the gentle hills around it. Inona startled when Delbin grabbed her wrist, tugging her gently to the left toward the sparsely forested slope.

"The house is back in the trees where this hill drops away," he said.

Inona nodded, and after a brief hesitation, she pulled her arm away. She might enjoy his touch, but she needed her hands free for battle. With a quick smile, she started forward, her senses ranging wide. She could feel nothing from Kien, nor had there been any energy surges that would indicate a mage at work.

Had he escaped the truck sooner than they'd thought?

She detected nothing on the way to the old house, a two-story wooden structure with sagging shutters and paint peeling from the siding. The farmhouse had clearly seen better days, and yet... Inona's eyes narrowed on a window beside the back door. A light.

With a gesture for Delbin to follow, she crept closer, only to jerk to a halt at the sound of a sharp bark. A dog? She scanned the area as Delbin froze beside her. There. Near the back corner, a dog was chained on a lead. The back door creaked open, and Inona strengthened the camouflage spell around herself and Delbin as a young man poked his head out.

"Hush, Ginger," the man called. "I'll be done in a few."

The man retreated, the door slamming behind him.

"Did you read him?" she asked Delbin.

"Yeah. He bought the place a few weeks back and is working on a remodel." Humor entered his mental voice. *"He's painting, so*

he left the dog outside. Seems he had to do a bit of cleanup last time he let Ginger in with him. Blue prints everywhere."

Inona grinned at the mental image Delbin had sent with the words. Then her smile dropped. *"Any hint of Kien?"*

"I don't think so. I didn't catch any thoughts about the dog barking sooner."

A sigh hissed through her teeth. *"Figures. Let's circle around to the truck."*

Quietly, they worked their way around the house and through the forest bordering the driveway. By the time the truck came into sight, Inona was ready to kick something. Kien could've gone anywhere, and there was little hope of tracking him without a team of her fellow scouts to search in multiple directions.

She couldn't take the time to hunt him herself. It was more vital to return to Moranaia with the information she'd gained about Kien's actions. How much of this did Lord Lyr know? All of the scouts had been warned to watch for Kien and to apprehend him if possible. But they'd been given no other details. Rumors swirled about a confrontation, but there'd been nothing about a spell to destroy Earth's energy. Regardless, this was too serious to assume Lyr knew about it.

Delbin leaned against the side of the truck, his steady regard focused on her. *"Well? What's next?"*

Inona bit her lip. She needed to return Delbin to his proper home. No matter what happened, he deserved to know what had befallen his brother.

"We should go," she sent to Delbin.

His eyes narrowed. *"Shouldn't we search a bit longer?"*

"Not alone," she answered with a shake of her head. *"I have to report in and gather more scouts."*

Delbin studied her for a moment, his expression inscrutable, and then nodded. *"When will you return?"*

She crossed her arms. *"You'll know firsthand. You're coming with me."*

Joy and dread collided within Delbin, and his heartbeat thumped hard in his ears as he stared at Inona. "I can't," he finally admitted.

"Excuse me?" she demanded.

He swallowed against the lump forming in his throat. "I was formally exiled. To return, I'll have to face the Myern's judgment, and I doubt he'll feel favorable toward me after our deception. Especially if I level with him about all of the rules here I've...bent."

Inona slid one knife back into her pocket. Then her hand darted out, her fingers wrapping around his wrist. "Did I give the impression that you have a choice?"

He froze, surprised by her hard tone. "Are you serious?"

"I believe you have information vital to Moranaia," she answered. She tightened her grip on his wrist. "Judgment or not, you're coming with me."

Damn. Well, he hadn't been that bad, right? He hadn't hurt anyone. He'd probably be sent straight back to Earth, but he hadn't done anything to warrant execution or an isolated exile. Hopefully. "I need to take the truck back to Grunge."

Inona shook her head. "We'll have to come back for that."

"No." She tugged at his wrist, but Delbin refused to budge. "I'm not going to cause Grunge trouble after all he's done for me. That guy back at the house will be leaving soon, and if he spots this truck, he'll have it towed. Maybe even call the police."

Wincing, she let go. "Fine. If he won't drive us back to the portal, we'll walk. But if this is a plan to cause trouble, I'll—"

"It's not." He smiled. "I promise I'll return with you."

"Let's go, then." Inona spun toward the truck. Then she paused, her hand on the edge of the truck bed as she peered over the side. "Hey, you don't happen to have a jar, do you?"

Delbin blinked. "A…jar?"

"Blood has power," she answered softly. "It's a dangerous thing, blood magic, but having a sample of Kien's could be useful for tracking."

A chill washed through Delbin. "Allafon was rumored to dabble in blood magic."

Inona eased closer and lifted her hand to Delbin's cheek. "I promise it isn't for that. I'd say it's a danger to leave the blood of a powerful mage where anyone can find it. We'll take the jar to Lord Lyr. He's honorable."

Was Lyr so trustworthy, then? Delbin had only met him a couple of times during his exile, before Lyr had stopped traveling to Earth to take his father's place as Myern. Delbin didn't know much about that, save that Lyr's father had died abruptly. He'd seemed kind and fair during their interactions. But more importantly, Inona trusted him.

"Let me see what I can find," Delbin said.

He gave her hand a squeeze and shifted away to search the clutter. There'd been a container full of Mason jars that Stephie had bought at a flea market for some craft project she'd seen on the Internet. Delbin moved a stack of bent metal poles and tossed aside the two old seat cushions beneath them. There. Quickly, he popped the latch securing the plastic box and lifted the lid just enough to snag a jar.

"Here it is," Delbin called out, lifting the Mason jar high.

Inona stepped closer to peer at the glass. "Is that writing on the side?"

Delbin turned it so he could see the side. Then he smiled. "It's just the name of the company that made the jar. Nothing mystical or anything."

"Ah." She considered the jar for a moment, then nodded. "It should work."

After he handed the jar over, Inona unscrewed the lid and leaned over the side of the truck. But she didn't scoop the blood in with her fingers as he'd expected. Instead, she waved her hand over the puddle, and Delbin's breath caught at the sudden surge of energy flowing over him. The blood pooled together and lifted, floating like water droplets in space. The eerie red bubbles dropped into the jar without a splash.

"Well, that trick certainly makes cleaning easier," he said as Inona secured the lid.

Despite the humor of the comment, she turned a serious glance his way. "You didn't see such magics on Moranaia?"

Delbin shrugged. "Other stuff, sure. But I don't remember that one. I was pretty young."

Inona's mouth tightened, but she didn't comment. Instead, she strode around the truck and jerked the passenger door open. Delbin smiled as he moved to his own door. He'd never had someone be so indignant on his behalf before. It was…nice. But he made certain his expression settled into something more neutral by the time he climbed into his seat. He had a feeling she wouldn't appreciate the observation.

7

Hardly an hour had passed before Delbin stood in front of the portal once again. Grunge had driven them back in his cargo van, and he'd even assured Delbin that he'd hold his place in the fair until Delbin knew if he'd be sent back to Earth. That was one relief, at least. As technology advanced, it grew more and more difficult to establish a new life.

"Are you ready?" Inona asked softly.

Delbin took a deep breath and nodded. He jolted as she twined her fingers with his, though both his body and heart warmed at the gesture. This was real. After all these years, he was finally going home. His shoulders straightened as he walked with Inona into the maelstrom of the Veil.

The mists flowed around them, so thick he could barely see his feet. But only for a moment. Energy poured from Inona into him, and he instinctively flinched as they seemed to leap forward into a swirl of color. Delbin closed his eyes

against a wave a dizziness at the abrupt movement. Had it been this way before? He'd been too terrified the first time to remember much.

After only a few heartbeats, it was over.

Delbin lifted a hand to his eyes against the sudden sunlight. Then the energy of Moranaia poured into him like hope. Oh, Gods.

A moan slipped from his lips as his power reserves were fully filled for the first time since his exile. He could feel his muscles strengthening, his magic expanding. His eyes slipped closed at the unexpected ecstasy.

Followed promptly by agony.

Voices crammed into his mind—too many to pick out words. He dropped Inona's hand to shove his palms against his temples, and he fell hard to his knees. What...?

Inona whispered to him from somewhere far away. Had she kept walking without him? "Delbin."

Gasping against the pain, he struggled to reinforce his ragged shielding. Too many. A crowd? "Get. Them. Away," he ground out.

"Who?" she asked softly. "There are only a couple of guards in the clearing."

A couple? But... Delbin poured more power into his mental shields. More layers to the invisible bubble of energy that guarded his mind. Slowly, the voices began to wink out. The pain to recede. His own thoughts became clear once more.

Had his talents grown so much since he'd left? They hadn't been overwhelming before, but he'd only been sixteen. He released a long breath and opened his eyes.

Inona knelt in front of him, her worried gaze focused on his face. "Are you okay?"

He blinked in surprise at her nearness. Hadn't she kept walking? It had certainly seemed like it. "I don't know what happened," Delbin answered. "But I think so."

He could feel the thoughts of others pounding against his shields, just outside the edge of "hearing." Delbin winced, and Inona's face wavered before his blurry eyes. He rubbed his forehead and blinked again to clear his vision. Why couldn't he control himself?

Gods, I wish I could hold him. I wish I had the right.

As Inona's voice rushed into his mind, Delbin jolted. They'd linked telepathically before, but it was obvious she hadn't meant him to hear this confession. What did she mean, she didn't have the right? A hint of her attraction had come through with her thoughts, so he wasn't sure what to think of her words. If only… But no. No way he would delve into her mind on purpose.

Her eyebrows drew together. "Are you sure you're fine?"

He shook his head to clear it. Now was not the time to focus on Inona's unwitting admission. Unfortunately. He added another layer of shielding between his mind and hers. "Yeah."

Delbin heaved himself to his feet, his body shaking as he took his first look at his home world in a hundred years. Sunlight trickled through the leaves of the huge trees that surrounded them, the branches sparser above the clearing where they'd paused. Two guards in leather armor stood by the stone portal, their faces impassive as they studied him.

But Delbin knew there were more in the trees, carefully camouflaged from sight—both tradition and his mind magic told him that.

Though his muscles trembled, Delbin forced himself to take a step forward. Then another. His rubber-soled boots made little sound against the packed dirt as he hobbled toward the edge of the clearing. He sensed Inona beside him, her voice the loudest as it pounded against his mental shields. Her worry picked at his protections until he feared they might crack.

"I'm okay," he murmured, risking a glance just in time to see her roll her eyes.

Inona's hand darted out, and she steadied him as his balance shifted. "Obviously."

Delbin paused at the edge of the clearing where it met the trail to the main estate. Heaving a sigh, he leaned against a nearby tree. Inona stared at him, her eyebrow lifted, but he only shrugged. How could he explain what he didn't understand? The initial surge of energy had made him feel stronger than he had in ages. So why was he shaky?

"It's fine to admit when you're overloaded," Inona said.

He blinked. "That's a thing?"

"I've never seen it in person, but I've heard of it," she answered. "You weren't ready for the full activation of your powers. Your body needs time to adjust, I think. But I'm no healer. There's one at the estate, *if* you can make it. Should I call ahead and have the healer's assistant carry you there?"

As he shoved himself away from the tree, Delbin caught the teasing glint in Inona's eyes. She'd challenged him on

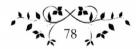

purpose, knowing perfectly well he wouldn't want such an undignified arrival. With an answering smirk, he started down the path. If he was heading to his own judgment, he'd damn well do it on his own two feet.

"Coming?" he called over his shoulder.

Grinning, she hurried to catch up.

By the time they reached the main entrance to the Myern's estate, Delbin had steadied somewhat—at least physically. He could walk without shaking, and greater vitality filled him with every breath. But even as he strengthened, his shielding grew closer to crumbling. With each step nearer to the manor, more voices pounded against his mind.

Moren had taken Delbin along the back trails to the portal when he'd started his exile, so he'd never actually seen Braelyn, Lyr's estate. Gods, what a sight. The tan stone structure curled around the trees like a snake—and almost as well camouflaged. From a distance, the rock's pattern blended with the nearby tree trunks, but as they neared the entrance, he could discern carvings of forest life. The entire place was a work of art.

But entirely too populated, a strain on Delbin's failing shields.

He rubbed at his temples in a vain attempt to ease the ache. Then he dropped his hands at Inona's concerned frown. "Just a bit of a headache," he whispered as a guard in leather armor opened the large wooden doors for them to enter.

Inona strode through without hesitation, but Delbin found himself stopping in the doorway. Was that a tree *inside* the house? The building had obviously curved around the forest, but he'd thought the trees had been…outside. But straight in front of him, a staircase wound around another huge trunk. He glanced to the left, and his breath caught at the even larger tree in its own alcove.

Eradisel.

He'd heard of the ancient sacred tree but had never been blessed enough to see it. Oria, his home estate, was not important enough to guard one of the nine trees. But then, Oria was nothing like this. The buildings were largely stone, the estate more like castles on Earth. Was this what the rest of Moranaia looked like? He'd left before that part of his schooling.

Inona took his hand in hers. "Would you like to visit Eradisel? There's an altar on the other side for private communion."

Delbin wanted to say yes as the tree's energy curled around him and a sense of peace washed through him. But he wanted even more to be done with the coming confrontation. "Maybe later," he answered.

With a nod, Inona led him past the staircase and to the right. He followed her through a winding hallway and tried not to stare at the intricate carvings decorating the walls. Gods, he could spend hours examining the forest scenes, so detailed he could see hints of animals peeking out around the trees. Why didn't Oria look like this?

Finally, they came to another, smaller door. A guard stood waiting, her midnight-black face impassive as she

studied them. "Welcome back, Inona. I hope this is worth the rush. Lord Lyr wasn't exactly pleased to be interrupted."

Inona smiled. "Trust me. He'll want to hear my news as quickly as possible."

"I hope you're right," the guard answered. "He has been under much stress lately."

"I'm sorry, Kera." Inona sighed, and Delbin glanced over in time to see her wince. "Now that you're acting as his assistant, it must be tough on you, too."

Kera merely shrugged. "It will ease, as all difficult things do."

As the guard turned to knock on the door, Inona released Delbin's hand and straightened. He understood why, since they were heading into a formal meeting, but the loss of contact saddened him. *Don't even think about going there with her,* he reminded himself. She was a Moranaian scout, and he was likely to be banished back to Earth. His attraction had no real future.

No matter how much he wished otherwise.

Kera opened the door and strode through, Inona following directly behind. Delbin shoved aside his musings and trailed them into yet another stunning room. He took in the sight of the large oval study, walls full of windows and bookcases, but his gaze halted on the elf standing impassively in front of a large desk. Lyrnis Dianore, Myern of the estate of Braelyn and all the Houses branching beneath—including Oria.

Delbin swallowed hard at the cold look on Lord Lyr's face. His expression meant nothing, a custom for formal

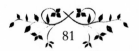

meetings, but a nervous lump formed in Delbin's throat. When Kera and Inona tapped fists to chests and bowed, he followed suit out of reflex, the motion slow and awkward. Dammit, what was wrong with him? He'd met Lyr on Earth without this level of anxiety.

But the elven lord had been dressed in Earth clothing, then, on Delbin's home turf. Not standing on a dais in a Moranaian tunic and pants. And Delbin's head hadn't been pounding with hundreds of barely blocked voices.

"Good afternoon, Myern," Kera said. "I have brought forth Inona and her charge, the exile Delbin."

Lord Lyr inclined his head. "Thank you, Kera."

The guard bowed again and turned away. As she strode toward the door where they'd entered, she gave Delbin a quick wink. He couldn't hold back the surprised grin that tipped his lips, but he smothered it as Lyr began speaking again.

"I regret that I do not have the leisure to linger over our discourse," the elven lord said, his gaze focused on Inona. "But I do trust that your family is well?"

Delbin blinked at the unexpected question, but Inona's voice held no surprise when she answered. "They are, Myern. As is yours?"

A slight smile crossed Lyr's lips. "My daughter is adjusting to life here quite well, and my new soulbonded is settling in. Even Kai is managing to stay out of trouble."

"Kai?" Delbin blurted.

Inona shot an annoyed glance at him over her shoulder. His memory of Moranaian manners caught up with him,

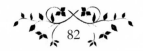

and Delbin winced. "Forgive the interruption. I'm too accustomed to Earth."

Surprisingly, the Myern laughed. "I get that a lot lately."

"I…" Delbin shook his head. "You do?"

"More than you can imagine," Lyr answered, his expression sobering. "You had a question about Kai?"

Delbin shifted in place, not certain he should pry. But what the hell? He was likely to be exiled anyway. "Did you mean Kaienan? You named him as family, but he is from Oria. Allafon's son."

Lyr gave a quick nod. "He recently bonded with my daughter, joining this House."

"Ah." Delbin's face heated, and suddenly he felt sixteen again. Manners for young elves had been more lax, and he'd barely begun to learn the intricacies of formal meetings when he'd been sent away. "Please forgive my forwardness, my lord."

Unexpectedly, the Myern relaxed, crossing his arms across his chest as he peered between Delbin and Inona. "Enough. What is this really about? An elf over three hundred years old should know how to handle a meeting like this despite being amongst humans for a century." Lyr's gaze settled on Delbin. "Talk."

Delbin's breath huffed out at the power behind the word, a mental command ringing alongside it. He faltered, grasping desperately for energy as his shields began to crumble. He needed help fast.

"Inona," he gasped.

"He's a telepath," she explained for him. "A strong one."

Pain built until his head seemed to be nothing but agony and other people's voices. Delbin's vision darkened, and he squeezed his palms against his temples. "Bad," he muttered as his knees buckled. Then even awareness winked out.

8

Inona darted toward Delbin, barely reaching him in time to keep him from falling onto his face. Her heart pounded in her ears as she turned him, lowering him to his back. He'd seemed to recover on their walk. To acclimate. Now this? She lifted her hand to his neck and let out a sigh at his steady pulse.

Lyr knelt beside them. "What happened?"

"I suspect it has to do with the energy here." Inona turned her head to meet Lyr's worried gaze. "When Lord Moren marked in the records that Delbin was more than three hundred, he lied. Delbin was a mere sixteen years old when he was exiled."

There was a heartbeat of silence as the Myern processed her words. Then his lips pinched tight and his nostrils flared. "Sixteen?"

Inona swallowed hard, though she hadn't been responsible for any of it. "Yes, Lord Lyr. And it seems

his talents weren't fully developed at the time. The greater magical energy of Moranaia hit him hard. He appeared to be getting better, but…"

Cursing, Lyr sprang to his feet and began to pace. Based on the expletives he muttered under his breath, she was quite happy *not* to be in Moren's position.

Delbin groaned softly, drawing her attention, and Inona peered at his features for any sign of stirring. But his eyes remained closed and his body motionless save his shallow breaths. What could she do? For that matter, why wasn't Lord Lyr doing anything? Her gaze flicked to the pacing Myern. It was unlike him not to take swift action.

The door opened, and the healer, Lial, rushed through, heading straight for Delbin and Inona. Without a word, the healer knelt next to Delbin and placed hands glowing blue with power around his head. Inona sat back, crossing her legs in front of her, and watched Lial work.

But when the glow faded and the healer looked up, Delbin still wasn't conscious. "I've called Ralan," Lial said.

Frowning, Lyr halted. "Why?"

"I was able to heal the slight damage caused by the abrupt overload, and I can shield him from being a danger to others," Lial explained. "But I can't teach a telepath of this strength to control himself. He's young, but he should know this already"

"Indeed," Lyr snapped. Then his gaze met Inona's. "What do you know of this?"

As they waited for Prince Ralan, Inona repeated what she'd learned about Delbin's growing powers and his attempt

to escape Allafon to save his family. "Lord Moren went to a great deal of trouble to hide the truth," she finally finished.

Jaw clenched, Lyr gave a sharp nod. She *really* didn't want to be Moren.

Lial's eyes glinted with fury when he spoke. "Delbin should be an apprentice at this age. If I get my hands on—"

"Not now, cousin," Ralan said as he strode into the room.

Inona's breath stuttered as the prince advanced. She'd seen him from a distance after he'd arrived on the estate, but she'd never met him in person. He'd been rumored as kind, if a bit arrogant, yet she couldn't help feeling a little intimidated as his gaze raked across her and down to Delbin.

Lyr's eyes narrowed. "Moren—"

"Did us a boon," Ralan interrupted again. As he sank to his knees, he glanced back at Inona. "Gathering Kien's blood was well done."

Inona shivered against a sudden chill. "How did you…?" Then she remembered his other talent. "I'm sorry. I forgot you are a seer."

The prince chuckled. "That's a rarity."

Before she could answer, Ralan's focus shifted to Delbin. Energy built in the room, but the pressure was gentle, like a gathering rain. No one spoke as several moments slid past. Then Delbin opened his eyes.

With a jerk, he bolted upright, his hands going to his temples. But he lowered them almost at once. "What…?"

Inona smiled, and as the tension eased from Delbin's shoulders, she found her own anxiety lessening. "You overloaded again," she said.

Blinking, he glanced at Lial and then Ralan. "Who are you?"

"He's the healer." A wicked grin crossed Ralan's face. "And me? I'm your new master."

Delbin's heart slammed hard. "Master?"

The man laughed.

"Good Gods, Ralan," Lyr said. "Stop playing around."

Ralan? The prince? He'd left Moranaia a few centuries ago, hadn't he? Delbin rubbed his hand across his forehead and prayed his head would clear. "Don't you live on Earth?"

"Not anymore," the prince answered, the humor fading from his expression. "And forgive my play on words. I couldn't resist. Master *is* the technical term for the person in charge of an apprentice, after all."

"Apprentice?" Dammit, what was wrong with him? His thoughts were fuzzy even though his mind was clear. No more voices—not even the whispers he'd grown accustomed to on Earth. Why was it harder to think in silence? "Not sure how that's going to work. Once you find out what I've done with my talents during my exile, I'm certain to be banished again."

A corner of Ralan's lips quirked. "Believe me, I did far worse."

"Is that so?" Lyr asked.

"I didn't hurt anyone," Ralan retorted with a shrug. "Much."

Confused, Delbin glanced at Inona. She smiled. "I don't think you're being re-banished."

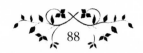

"I hadn't had time to consider it," Lyr said. "But it appears Prince Ralan has decided for us."

For a moment, Delbin could only sit in shock, his gaze flicking between Lyr and the prince. It couldn't be that easy. A century of deception forgiven with little debate? For that matter, did he want to stay? All those years dreaming of Moranaia, and now that he was here, he could barely function. He didn't even know if he still had family.

Before anything else, he had to find out.

"Could you tell me..." Delbin took a bracing breath. "Do you know what happened to my brother? Inona said she'd heard nothing of him."

"There was nothing about a brother in your records." Lyr's lips pursed in thought. Then he frowned. "Wait. Your family name is Rayac. For some reason, that sounds familiar, but I... Ah, *clechtan.*"

Time seemed to slow as Delbin prepared to ask what he didn't want to recognize. But he *had* to know. "What is it?"

"There was a Tenic Rayac among the list of those killed during the final confrontation with Allafon." Lyr's face softened with pained sympathy. "He was...not on our side."

His brother on Allafon's side? Delbin's hands tightened into fists. "Not possible."

The Myern's nostril's flared. "You believe I would lie about such a thing?"

"No, but you must be mistaken." Chest growing tight, Delbin shoved himself to his feet. He wavered as dizziness hit, and Inona reached out to steady him. But he couldn't

look at her. "I left Moranaia to save him. My mother would have told him that. Why would he have betrayed us?"

"It seems we have much to ask Moren," Lyr answered sharply. "But I assure you I am not mistaken. I tend to remember the names of those who try to kill me."

Moren had visited Earth more than once in the last century to ensure Delbin's safety. Wouldn't he have given some hint? But Lord Lyr was by all accounts an intelligent and fair person. He didn't have a reputation for repeating falsehoods, and what reason would he have to do so? Though Delbin's stomach lurched with guilt, he found himself leaning toward belief. Against his own brother.

"If it's true, the bastard Moren lied to me," Delbin said. "Just a few years ago, he told me my family was fine."

Averted gazes and resounding silence rammed the truth home.

His heartbeat thumped a frantic pace in his ears, and his vision went hazy. Gods, he still remembered the first time he'd held his baby brother. Those chubby cheeks and that new baby smell. He'd been willing to do anything for Tenic. He *had* done anything. He'd sacrificed friendships, education, reputation—his entire world. All for *nothing*.

Fury overtook reason, and power shot from Delbin like the fist he wanted to smash into a wall.

Only to slam into a shield not his own, a bubble of energy placed around him by someone else. The magic rebounded with a soft crack, and Delbin stumbled back at the return punch. Stifling a curse, he rubbed at his aching

head. But he'd deserved it. He could cause others real pain by forcing his thoughts and emotions into their minds, and it didn't matter if it was intentional or not. He would still be responsible.

Delbin took a deep breath and forced down the worst of his turmoil. Sometime soon, he'd find a private place to free his emotions and let loose his rage. Instead, he turned to face the source of the new shield surrounding him.

Ralan smirked again. "Best shield ever for teaching control."

"Maybe I don't want to be your apprentice," Delbin said.

The prince shrugged. "You'll be free of me sooner than you realize."

An odd note in Ralan's tone had Delbin peering at him, but if there'd been some cryptic meaning beneath the statement, there was no sign of it on Ralan's face. "You think I'll be a quick study?" Delbin finally asked.

This time, the prince's smile held no hint of teasing. "You'll have to be."

Delbin wanted to ask for clarification, but he knew better. Seers were enigmatic for a reason, and there were some things he'd rather not know. "I guess we'll find out."

"Well, it'll have to be without me," the healer said. "I've other work to do."

Delbin's mouth fell open as the healer spun away and marched from the room without another word. He'd heard of bad bedside manner, but damn. Delbin glanced around the room, but none of the others appeared shocked. Maybe this was normal behavior? He couldn't remember much about the elderly healer at Oria.

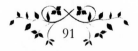

Inona placed a hand on his forearm, and for a moment, a hint of her feelings slipped through his shielding again. Not just attraction this time but also protectiveness. His eyes shot to hers, but he saw no sign of such feelings there. Was he mistaken, or was her reaction to him simply not something she intended to pursue? Too bad he didn't have time right now to find out.

"Don't worry about Lial," she said. "He's been crankier than usual lately."

"We've all had cause," Lyr said. Then he straightened. "I'm not sure what Inona told you about Allafon's betrayal, but we've all dodged death more than once. And it all goes back to Kien. He controlled Allafon for quite some time in an attempt to get me out of the way."

Inona's fingers tightened on Delbin's arm as she turned to the Myern. "Forgive me for failing to capture him," she said.

Lyr shook his head. "You were not equipped for such a mission."

"It's for me to do," Ralan said, his voice going harsh. "And only me."

There was a hint of something—a thought or feeling—that hit Delbin with the prince's words, but it dangled just out of reach. Like a memory he couldn't quite grasp. But Delbin couldn't help the pique of curiosity. Was Ralan hiding something about Kien? From the hard glint in Ralan's gaze, Delbin decided it was another thing he didn't want to know.

There was already enough he needed to clarify.

"I'd like to know my status here. If you think only you should confront Kien, why bring me on as an apprentice?"

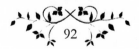

A memory of his baby brother, laughing in their mother's arms, filled Delbin's mind and brought a lump to his throat. His fists clenched. "I have plenty of my own reasons to go after Kien."

"Control your power," Ralan bit out as Delbin's anger surged. "We'll discuss this later."

Lyr crossed his arms. "Hiding stuff again?"

Ralan gave Lyr an irritated glance. "It's a matter of timing. And to answer what Delbin really wants to know… We'll stay here until his magic is stabilized. Then he'll return to Earth."

Well, didn't that just figure? Delbin ground his teeth together. "So much for not banishing me."

"You'll never be exiled again," Ralan said in an absent tone. "But I'm not certain you'll ever live here."

A shiver captured Delbin, and his eyes snapped up. He shouldn't ask. But he couldn't stop himself. "Death?"

Ralan blinked as though returning to himself. "I wasn't talking about death. When all of this is over, you'll have to decide where you belong. The choices may be broader than you think."

Delbin snorted. "Clear as mud."

"What?" Inona asked.

Lyr also looked puzzled, but Ralan chuckled. "An Earth saying. Trust me, it's sometimes just as hazy and frustrating for me."

Trust me. How many people had said that to him over the last century? Delbin straightened. "There's a lot of faith expected from me and little done to earn it."

Ralan waved a hand. "You know I was using that loosely."

"I do," Delbin answered. "And I'll work as your apprentice. But you're right when you say I'll have decisions to make. At this point, I have no idea where I belong. Trust? After Moren lying to me about my family, I'm not sure when I'll find that kind of certainty again."

Beside him, Inona shifted back, a subtle retreat. Did she think he spoke of her? In the short time he'd known her, she'd done more than anyone save Grunge to earn his trust. She'd believed in him, championed him. But with the others looking on, he couldn't explain without embarrassing her. Inona held her feelings too close for that.

Shoulders slumping, Delbin ran his hand through his hair. "Is there a place I can rest?"

9

Delbin leaned against the window frame and stared into the forest. It was so strange here after a century in the human world, especially in modern times. No rush of cars on roads, no shouts—none of the countless noises of life that made their own human symphony. Sometimes, he'd catch an echo of a voice or a child's laughter from the ground below his tower window. Mostly there was only the hissing of leaves brushing together in the breeze, birdsong, and the chittering of small forest creatures.

Somehow, Earth forests never seemed so still.

He'd done nothing but stare outside in the hour since he'd been shown to his room, a round chamber beneath Ralan's. The guard, Kera, had said Lyr's bonded had stayed here for a brief time after her arrival. A lady from Alfheim, home of the light elves. Delbin grinned. He knew a couple of pagans who'd lose their shit if they met one of the

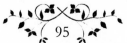

Ljósálfar of Norse legend. Not that the humans knew what Delbin truly was. He'd trusted no one with that.

He settled his forehead against the window frame and closed his eyes. What was he going to do? Delbin had longed for home for so many years, but now that he was here, it felt foreign. Yet the human world wasn't really better. He could never let anyone too close without fearing they'd discover the truth about him. Humans couldn't get past their own tiny differences. What chance did elves have of living an open, peaceful life on Earth?

None.

A knock sounded. Delbin shoved away from the window and spun to face the door. He sent out a delicate mental probe to see who was there and then cursed to find Ralan's shield inhibiting his powers. Great. With a scowl, Delbin marched to the door and jerked it open. Inona's stunned face greeted him.

"Is it a bad time?" she asked.

Delbin ran his hand through his hair and forced himself to settle. "Not really. I'm just on edge right now. And tired of feeling helpless."

She canted her head. "Helpless?"

"Why don't you come in?" Delbin asked instead of answering. No need for an audience if anyone happened to be nearby.

Though Inona peered at him curiously, she shrugged and strode into the room. She waited until he'd closed the door to speak. "Is there some kind of secret?"

"Nah. Just my own embarrassment." Delbin gave a sheepish smile. "I was annoyed because of Ralan's shield

96

around me. I feel like I have no control over myself. Like a kid whose parents don't want him to cause mischief with his magic."

"Ralan seems like a good judge of character."

Delbin's mouth dropped. Was that some kind of dig? Her expression held no sign of humor. "One hundred and sixteen might be young yet, but I promise you I—"

"Oh, stop," Inona said. Then she started laughing. "That was too easy."

"You—" He snapped his mouth closed. Inona was teasing him? Yeah, he needed to take advantage of that. "Ah well, you might be old, but you brought my troublemaking self here. I guess you can't say much."

She tapped her foot. "Old? I'm four hundred and eighty-nine, not five thousand."

"Wow, over three hundred years older than I am." Delbin grinned. "I can't believe I'm attracted to someone so ancient."

Her expression went blank at his words, and he realized what he'd just confessed.

Damn.

A strange blend of hope and fear froze Inona in place. He was truly attracted to her? Gods, she wanted nothing more than to act on that. But Delbin might not return to Moranaia for good. She couldn't fall for someone else who would have to leave, even if it would be willing this time.

"I can't stand uncertainty," she whispered.

Delbin rubbed the back of his neck. "What? Where did that come from?"

"I've had my own trouble with upheaval." Inona let out a sigh. Should she reveal the whole sad truth? "I want to get to know you better, but with your life so uncertain, I'm not sure I should."

Delbin stared, face slack with shock. Then he ran his hand through his hair again, leaving the blond strands tumbled in disarray. "Did someone hurt you?"

"He wasn't my soulbonded, but I loved him," Inona found herself confessing. She swiped at her suddenly wet cheeks, and her face heated at the show of weakness. "We'd only been together for a couple of years when a feud started with a neighboring estate. Keth was a minor lord, his holdings small, but he had ambition. Against orders, he retaliated against the other family in hopes of consolidating power."

Delbin's brow rose. "Just like that?"

"It really did seem to be out of nowhere." She lowered her gaze. "To this day, I don't know why he chose such a thing. Although I suppose he was never the same after his mother's death."

Delbin stepped closer and brought his hands to her shoulders. "You shouldn't blame yourself."

Inona's eyes shot up. "I—"

"I mean it," he said. "I know what it's like to look back and wonder. But I've been in enough minds to know that there's no changing people. Even when you can control them, coerce them. In the end, only they can change themselves."

Her lips twisted. "Not something Keth seemed interested in. Gods, what a mess that was. After his exile, I spent a solid decade wandering Moranaia. It was a while before life felt solid again."

"Inona…" Delbin slid his hands down her arms and twined his fingers with hers. "I get it. I do. But I suppose I'm too used to being around humans. I've seen so many of them live and die in such a short space of time, and it's taught me to take happiness where I can. If you're not interested, I understand, but I'd hate to lose this chance to be with you."

Could it be that simple? She'd held on to so much hurt for so long, forever cautious of those around her. Yet here she was, caught in the middle of a royal plot with a man she would have dismissed as a criminal. Maybe it was time to let go, at least a little.

Suddenly, Delbin smirked. "Hey, don't forget I could get offed by Kien. I'd at least like to have dinner with you first."

An unexpected laugh slipped free. "I suppose we can do that."

Delbin tugged her closer, and she let herself settle against him. As his arms wrapped around her waist, he gave a questioning glance. Inona stared into his eyes for a moment and then nodded. Yes. Even their long lives were too short to squander happiness.

He lowered his head, and his lips brushed hers. Soft and tentative as an early spring breeze. Inona's eyes slid closed, and her sigh mingled with his breath. It was bliss to be held

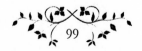

like this, a luxury she rarely allowed herself. It was time she allowed herself more. Her hands slid to his cheeks as she rose up.

And took the kiss deeper.

When Inona finally pulled away, they were both out of breath. Delbin eyed the bed and bit back a groan. Nope. No way she was ready for that. Hell, he didn't know if he was. He closed his eyes and lowered his forehead to hers. So much in his life was uncertain, but he was sure of one thing. He wanted to get to know Inona better.

He found a slow smiled curving his lips as he leaned back to meet her gaze. "Do you think we'll be able to stay out of trouble long enough for that dinner?"

She chuckled. "After the kind of day we've had, I'm not taking a guess."

A knock sounded at the door, and Delbin stifled a curse. Once again, he couldn't scan the person on the other side. Normally, he'd have seen if he could ignore the knock and follow the urge to kiss Inona again. Annoying shielding.

He marched to the door and jerked it open, only to find a scowling Ralan on the other side. "I'm rather occupied," Delbin said.

"I can tell," the prince replied sharply. "I'd appreciate if you'd stop projecting."

Delbin's frown deepened. "What are you talking about? You have me locked down."

"From everyone but me," Ralan grumbled. His expression would have been amusing if Delbin wasn't so annoyed. "It's my shield, so there's a link. Cut it out."

Delbin stared at the prince for a moment. Then humor won out over annoyance, and he laughed. "Sorry."

"I can see how sympathetic you feel," Ralan said, though his expression had lightened.

"I suppose we should get to work." Delbin glanced back at Inona. "After dinner."

Ralan waved a hand, and a smile twisted his lips. "I suppose I'll be generous. I'll get back to you later."

As the prince departed, Delbin turned back to Inona. He felt somehow lighter, as though the darkness of his brother's betrayal, a brother he'd never even had the chance to know, had been at least a little counteracted. There was pain, but there was also hope. He had no idea what would happen when he helped Ralan hunt down Kien—whether the prince wanted him there are not.

But for the moment, Delbin was alive. The future would tend to itself.

The following short story first appeared in the anthology Against All Odds. It wasn't written as part of The Return of the Elves series and has no direct connection, although it could exist in the same universe. Who knows? Maybe the Eiana will pop up again.

The Grove
Between

Faen perched on the edge between dimensions, two worlds unfolding before him. The tree where he crouched was rooted in his own world, but a different meadow hazed his vision. The pale colors, so much less vibrant than his forest, had his blood thrumming. Such an odd land, this other world. What better place to greet each dawn?

But then *she* appeared, and he almost fell from his tree.

Black hair whipped in a tangle behind the woman as she ran for the safety of the forest, straight for where he perched. Faen's hands gripped the nearest branch to keep his balance. *A human.* Few dared to come to the glade, and none while he'd been around. Much to his perpetual disappointment.

She lifted the pale fabric of her gown high as she ran, and a bright purple cloak streamed behind her. Flashes of color gleamed from the purple, but she was too far away to make out details. Still, it was enough. Only the most important of her people wore such rich garments. But why would this high-born woman be running across the meadow at dawn?

1

A rumbling bark cracked across the meadow from behind her, followed by another. Then a storm of them. Faen squinted at the horizon. Hounds—and not normal ones, either. Someone had sent spirit hounds after her. His muscles tightened for action even as he puzzled over the dilemma. He wasn't forbidden from moving between realms, but it was discouraged. And she was human. Possibly dangerous—maybe even a criminal.

But mothers' blood, he couldn't leave her to die.

As she neared, her gaze focused on the trail just beside his tree. The path that led to the grove where her people had once called upon his own. Faen winced. She would receive no help there, not since a long-ago lord of her people had declared the *Eiana* to be *yonaiee*, foul demons who brought misfortune and ruin. The queens of the *Eiana* had never forgotten the slight.

The dull thud of her feet sounded between the frantic barking of the dogs. The woman cast a look over her shoulder, then stumbled, a wail of despair slipping free. Faen held his breath as she righted herself, but they both knew she'd never outrun the hounds. Fear pinched her amber-gold face as her gaze lit upon his tree.

For a moment, Faen thought she'd seen him, though that was impossible. He was too much in his own world. But as the hounds streamed across the meadow behind her, she looked up again and let her cloak drop in a rich, purple heap. Birds. Blue and green birds danced with golden streamers, woven painstakingly into the cloth. High-born indeed.

The woman pulled the back of her gown up between her legs and slipped it into her broad sash. With one last glance at the hounds, she gripped a low-hanging branch near the bottom of the tree and began to climb. Her soft-soled shoes slipped against the bark and her arms visibly trembled, but fear drove her up to stand on the lowest branch.

Five of the hounds reached the base of the tree. Their dark eyes fastened on the woman as they circled, snarling. Wary, Faen made no sound as he crept down the trunk of the tree. Though she couldn't hear him, the spirit hounds might, and he'd rather not fight them with her in between. They couldn't enter easily into his world, but the between-space that separated his realm from hers? That was fair game.

One of the hounds leapt for the woman's feet, snapping just a breath away, as Faen grew closer. He'd never reach her in time if she didn't start climbing again. A second hound leapt, and the woman cried out as its snout grazed her foot. Spurred into action, she turned to scramble farther up the tree. But her feet kept slipping against the bark, and her arms shook so hard the branch she'd grabbed rattled. Each finger's length she gained took forever.

Why didn't the hounds go for the kill?

A long growl rumbled out from below moments before the first hound jumped for her again. She jolted at the sound, her body ramming into the trunk of the tree, and the hasty tuck of her skirt slipped free to tangle around her feet. She cast her hand around frantically for the higher branch she'd been seeking, but as the dog fastened on her skirt, she

3

grasped only air. One good tug, and she'd fall.

Faen wrapped his legs around the branch above her and leaned over, materializing his hand in her realm just moments before he touched her. Her brown eyes snapped up at the contact, and a scream ripped from her throat. But he didn't have time to wonder why. With a heave, he pulled her up. With a stretch of his magic, he shifted her to his world.

Mio couldn't help it—she screamed.

Her vision went gray, so deep it almost faded to black. Was she dreaming? Dead? The painful pounding of her heart in her chest belied the latter. Then a tingle shuddered through her, passing like a spark from the crown of her head all the way to her toes before blinking away. All at once, her vision was clear.

A hand pressed against her mouth, cutting off the scream still pouring from deep within. Mio choked the sound down as a face came into view. A face—and the body attached to the hand. Her gaze darted around, then, and her breath seized. The bright forest spun around her as he lifted her in front of him. This was not her world. It couldn't be.

Could he be *Eiana?*

Mio studied him, considering. According to legend, the Forest People looked much like her own kind, their skin perhaps a deeper shade of gold—almost bronze—and their cheekbones a bit higher. Eyes a little rounder. He was certainly all of that. But her people had once intermarried

with the *Eiana*, before magic was forbidden. He wasn't so foreign-looking that she could know for sure. But his clothing? That marked him more absolutely than his features. Tight but soft-looking leather outlined his muscles as they flexed, keeping her steady in front of him. Leaves danced through the braid of his black hair. None of her people would dress so.

Mio shivered as she met his moss-green eyes. "If you intend to do me harm, you might as well send me back to the hounds."

"Harm?" He asked, his voice lilting softly. "Why would I save you just to hurt you?"

She shrugged. "My uncle has no qualms about it."

"The one who sent the spirit hounds?"

"Yes," Mio answered. "Though he won't kill me yet. Maybe it would be better if you *did* wish me harm."

His eyes narrowed on her face for a long moment. "Sent to capture, then. What could a high-born lady like *you* have done?"

"I have your blood in my veins." Her mouth pinched tight. "That is enough."

He pushed back against the tree trunk, the quick motion shaking their branch. "I am but nineteen turnings. No one has my blood, I assure you."

"Not *you*," Mio muttered, though a thread of humor slipped through. "Your people, I meant. The *Eiana*. Our family still carries the blood."

The man let out a soft whistle. "I knew humans hated us, but I didn't know it has gone so far that our lineage would earn someone death. At least not here."

5

"Only amongst the Devout."

Mio let out a startled yelp as his hands tightened on her arms. He released her, his expression crestfallen, then reached out to steady her again before she could topple. "Forgive me. I've heard rumors of the Devout. Fanatics plaguing our cousins to the north."

She gripped her hands around the branch so hard her knuckles went pale. "They grow more powerful. My father held out, but…"

Mio took a deep breath, then finally braved a glance at the ground. But there were no spirit hounds here. Nothing but a mossy forest floor. Biting her lip, she looked back up into his eyes. "Why did you bring me here?"

A smile stretched slowly across his face. "I have no idea."

"The *Eiana* haven't been seen around here in a couple of generations. I'd hoped if I could just make it to the glade…" Her gaze drifted to his chin. "I know they—you—have stopped answering, but I had to try. This isn't the glade, though. And you don't look like a noble."

"Absolutely not." His laugh shivered through her like the tingle that had brought her here. "I'm in training with the guard, not as a dignitary."

"Might I have your name?"

"Faen," he answered. "Faen of the Oaken."

She gave a soft smile. "I am Mio, Lady of Kioku."

His brows rose. "*The* Lady?"

Mio twisted her arms, a subtle hint for him to release her, and straightened as best she could as soon as he did. "Yes. I was my father's sole heir. I became Lady of Kioku a

few moons ago upon his passing. No matter how much my step-uncle contests it."

"My condolences."

Before she could answer, another tingle flowed through her, and Faen let out a soft curse. Her heart pounding in her throat, Mio leaned to the side, following Faen's gaze to the base of the tree. A spark of light trembled there, the faint outline of a hound lifting its ghostly snout to the sky. Mio shoved her hand against her mouth to stifle a cry.

"Easy, now," Faen murmured as he pointed his hand, palm-first, at the hound below. A few whispered syllables and a flash of light, and the spirit form was gone. Even still, her breath came in frenzied gasps.

"How did it get here?" she managed to get out.

A frown furrowed Faen's brow. "Your uncle—or whoever—summoned stronger spirits than I've ever seen. We need to move from this place."

Though her body trembled, Mio nodded. "Will you take me to your queen?"

Faen's eyes widened. "What?"

"Your queen?" Mio said, her tone wry. "I assume you still follow one?"

With a shake of his head, Faen rose, but the branch barely shifted beneath them. "I can't take you straight to the queen. Do you *want* to die? It might have been generations ago, but the slight your people dealt to her house has not been forgotten."

Mio eased herself along the branch, only to halt as she began to waver. Scowling, she looked up into his eyes. "Not

the people of *my* lands. The king had fallen in with the Devout. We thought the worst over, but—"

Shock cut off her words as another form appeared below. Muttering again, Faen dispelled it, then held out his hand. "Come on. I can get us out of here, if you'll let me."

She hesitated for only a breath before slipping her hand into his. "Do it."

Faen pulled the lady to her feet, then paused to study her. Her whole body trembled as she fought to stay standing, and she gripped his hand so tightly it was beginning to ache. Brave she might be, but equipped for an escape through the trees she wasn't. "I can carry you a few trees over if you'll allow it."

Her eyes widened. "We aren't climbing down now?"

"Too close to the rift between our dimensions," Faen answered with a shrug.

"Normally, this would not be allowed, but—" Lady Mio stood tall even as she wavered on the branch. "As you've pointed out, we aren't on my land. So carry me without fear of death."

Even as he shook his head in exasperation, Faen pulled her tight against him. He'd heard about how the humans treated their noble women but hadn't been sure he believed it. No man but their mates could touch them—not even the slightest brush. As Faen used his free arm to pull them higher up the tree, he wondered at the tales.

Was he the first man to touch her since she reached womanhood, or did she have a mate?

With a grunt, Faen swung them both to the broad branch of a nearby oak, then dashed along it until he reached the trunk. Lady Mio's arms tightened around his waist at the quick movement, but she made no protest. Not even when he jumped a step down to an intersecting limb. She might not be physically strong, but her will held as firm as the finest sword.

When he reached the edge of the grove, Faen descended. Eight stones ringed the clearing—symbols of the eight sacred directions—to seal the spells of protection. Here, of all places, they would be safe, for surely the spirit hounds would not be able to move past the stones in her world. As the formal linking place between dimensions, once used often and with joy, the spells set here were ancient and powerful. At least they should be.

Faen stopped in the center, but he didn't let the lady go. Warm and soft where she pressed against him, she felt so right. His throat tightened as he looked at her. She was so beautiful, from the brown of her eyes to the fall of black hair snarling around them. But more, her spirit. Her soul shone back at him like a star.

"Faen!"

The voice snapped him from his reverie. Wincing, Faen released Lady Mio, took a deep breath, and turned. "Good morn, father."

Mio stiffened at Faen's words. *This* was his *father?* The man who stood tall at the edge of the grove, his rich, blue

robes marking him a noble and mage? What game did Faen play, calling himself a warrior? She'd heard enough stories of the *Eiana* to know that noble sons rarely entered such a dangerous profession, especially if gifted.

And she'd seen Faen use magic with her own eyes.

"Father?" she choked out. Gods, had she fallen into worse trouble? She'd run from one deception straight into another.

"When he claims me," Faen answered with a shrug.

But Mio caught the pain underpinning his words and relaxed just a little. If there was a rift between the two, then maybe he hadn't lied. She hoped he hadn't. She felt drawn to him—so safe in his arms. Though she hadn't been touched by any man since turning twelve summers, she couldn't recall ever feeling so before.

The noble stepped closer, his brow pinched. "What have you done, Faen?"

"Saved a life."

"Rifts are not to be opened without permission."

Faen's hands clenched. "There is no formal law, only tradition. I'll not see a woman mauled by spirit hounds while I stand by."

"Spirit hounds?" The noble swayed as though he'd been pushed, and his wide eyes flicked to Mio. "Like the ones in the north?"

"Just so," Faen answered.

The noble stared hard at Mio. "You brought those foul things to our land?"

"Not I." Mio stood tall, refusing to back down. "I am Mio, Lady of Kioku. A man from the north tries to coerce

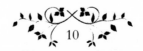

me into marriage so he can steal my place. When I escaped, he called upon the hounds."

"Still, you ran them here."

A spark of anger burned hot beneath her breast. "I have come to call upon the *Eiana* in the ancient way."

The man moved closer, almost close enough to touch. Though he tried to cow her with his gaze, Mio held firm. This was more important than her life. "Your people lost that right long ago," he finally said.

"The lord who insulted your queen was removed by his own brother, my great-grandfather, for the dishonor he dealt." Mio's voice went cool. "Which your people would know had you not ignored all attempts at communication."

The noble smirked. "We are happy enough to leave you to yourselves."

"That is not in the spirit of our treaty."

"Nevertheless, our queen's word is law."

Mio took a deep breath and forced her trembling limbs still. Tilting her chin up, she lifted a brow. "Is it not true that any of the *Eiana* might have counsel with the queen?"

"I…" The noble shifted, a hint of unease lining his face. "Of course they may."

"Then take me to her by right of my blood," Mio said. "As my great-grandmother was her own cousin."

Faen couldn't hold back a smile as Lady Mio's words settled into silence. He glanced over his shoulder, and his breath caught at how regal she stood, spine straight and

head held high. Never mind the creases and smudges on her white gown or the long hair tangled around her arms. Though she couldn't be much older than him—might even be younger—he felt certain she ruled the Kioku absolutely.

"Well," his father answered, his voice taut with fury. "That does present a problem. No provision has been made for such an occurrence, and as such, I am afraid I must consult the queen."

Faen whipped back around to face his father. "Do not treat her poorly because she arrived here with me."

Cold blue eyes met Faen's green. "Your presence means less than nothing, save the breaking of our laws."

It shouldn't hurt. After ten years, it shouldn't. But it did. Faen stiffened against the feeling, willing all sign of the pain from his face. He'd known when he'd made his choice that some rifts could never be healed. "With blood of the *Eiana* in her veins, I have broken nothing."

"That remains to be seen," his father snapped. "You will remain in the grove of her world until I return with an answer. Do not think to leave."

Faen snorted at that—like his father would venture past the sacred circle in her dimension to hunt them down—but said nothing as magic shivered through him. A blink, and his father was gone. Faen stumbled against a shift in the ground beneath his feet, but righted himself quickly. The grass here was paler, the trees smaller. And the rumbling barks of the hounds more than alarming.

Slipping a knife from his belt, Faen moved close to Lady Mio as his gaze swept the perimeter of the grove. With each count, a curse slipped free. Ten spirit hounds. He could take on one, maybe two or three, but if all of them breached the circle, he and Mio would be dead. Did the mages reinforce the warding spells on this side?

Two of the hounds jumped toward them, thudding against the protections, and the shudder that raced through Faen gave him his answer. It would hold, but not forever. Not if all of the hounds worked as one.

"Why are you not among the nobles?" Lady Mio murmured.

A wry laugh slipped free as he looked at her. "I have no wish to be. My magic is too small to place me above menial, and I don't enjoy spellwork enough to make that worthwhile. I would much rather guard the forest. My mother is at peace with my decision, but…" Faen let out a sigh. "My father will never accept it."

"I'm sorry." Grief pinched the skin around Mio's eyes. "My own father loved me. He tried to see me wed before he died, but I thought his fears about my step-uncle were unfounded. Little did I know."

Faen lifted a hand but dropped it a breath away from her face. He couldn't touch her casually. He shouldn't have touched her at all, even to save her—and not just because of her laws. She did something to him. Twisted his insides and made his heart throb almost painfully in his chest. But he could never have her. Not the Lady of Kioku.

"Tell me more?" he dared to ask.

Mio shuddered as one of the hounds knocked against the protection spell, but her gaze didn't waver. "My grandfather's

second wife was a widow from the north. She brought her young son, and they seemed to settle in well enough. But their clan believes that the Lord and Lady of War should be prime among the gods, not the Lord and Lady of the Light. When my grandfather died, she and her son returned north to join the Devout."

"The Devout believe in the same gods as your people?" Faen asked in surprise.

"Yes, just not the order of ascendance."

"Then why—"

"Why do they disavow magic?" Lady Mio shook her head. "The Lord and Lady of War detest it, preferring physical combat. The Lady of Light is magic itself, so that hatred is rarely felt while She rules. Except where the Devout hold sway. I thought we'd rid ourselves of their influence, and I'd believed my step-uncle had long forgotten us. I was wrong."

Faen remembered her earlier words. "He's trying to force you into marriage?"

"Many of my people have the blood of the *Eiana* from all our years of intermixing," Mio said. "He threatened to call upon the armies of the Devout to wipe us out if I don't wed him. But I know well enough that he'd kill me not long after the vows were said."

The hounds' snarling growls faded away as Faen considered her. No matter what the queen might answer, he had to help Lady Mio. The Devout taking a stronghold near his lands would be reason enough, it was true. But he cared little for that. Faen might not be able to have her, but he'd die to save her. A shaky laugh strangled free from his throat. All for a woman he'd just met.

Mio's eyes went wide. "Are you unwell?"

"Probably." But a grin slipped across his lips. "Just considering my demise."

"What?"

Faen fought against the urge to touch her. "Because there's no way in any world I'll let someone hurt you."

Mio sucked in a breath at Faen's words. He felt such for her? Most men feared her, for the Lady's reign was absolute. They served her, yes, and would die for her if she were attacked. But not for herself. She'd been Lady for such a short time, and at barely eighteen summers, she'd yet to earn her people's love and respect.

Duty was a poor substitute.

Yet here was Faen, an emotion in his eyes she hardly dared guess. It couldn't be love or even affection. Surely not so soon. But Divine Light, how it made Mio's heart pound! Trembling, she lifted her hand. Her fingers shook as they hovered a hairsbreadth from his cheek. Did she dare? No noblewoman of her people would.

Mio stood taller, and her trembling faded. She was Lady of Kioku. She would touch whomever she wished.

The pads of her fingers brushed across his cheek, and Faen stilled, his eyes going wide. Mio shivered at the feel of him. His skin, so warm and soft. She longed to curl up against him and settle her head against his chest. To just

be held. But even as Lady, that would be too much. With a sigh, she pulled her hand back and cupped it to her chest. Savoring.

"My lady?" Faen asked, voice soft though his eyes flared with heat.

"I shouldn't have," Mio whispered. "Forgive me. But if I'm to die—"

Faen took a step closer, but he didn't touch her. "You will *not*."

"If the queen doesn't offer aid, the odds are not good."

A familiar magic trembled around them for a moment before Faen's father appeared, his eyes going hard as he looked between them. "You reach too far if you think to have a noblewoman. Not since giving up your own place."

Mio stiffened. "There is more to nobility than wielding magic."

"For you." The noble made a small gesture, and for the first time, Mio noticed the soldier standing behind him. Her stomach pitched as the man dropped a pack on the ground, and she fought the urge to bite her lip as she looked back to Faen's father. "If you treated mages more highly, perhaps you wouldn't have spirit hounds chasing you, hmm?"

"I take it the queen refused to see her?" Faen asked before Mio could bite out an insult.

"Her majesty requests time to consider the matter." The noble waved his hand at the pack. "I will return with her answer in two days' time. But as she is ever generous, she bid me leave you with some defenses."

The soldier stepped forward again to prop a bow and a quiver of arrows against the pack. But no sword. Mio's eyes narrowed. "How very gracious."

"More gracious than instant death," Faen's father answered. "And Faen? You are but one misstep from exile. Remember it well."

Her gaze locked on the bow, Mio barely noticed the thrill of power as the noble and his guard left. The hounds, still and watching in the presence of the mage, set to howling. Mio shivered. No aid, at least not in time. No warriors to help eliminate her step-uncle. She sank to her knees, heedless of the stains she ground into her gown. Heedless of everything.

Faen knelt before her, blocking her view of the pack. "Mio? My lady?"

She shook her head, trying to work herself free from despair. Despair stole strength, and it was strength Mio needed. "I don't know what to do."

"We fight," Faen answered. His gaze caught hers. "Is there any other choice?"

Mio thought of her people. Their downcast eyes as they darted around the castle, their fear of her step-uncle almost palpable. The little girls with their faces pressed against the window of a cottage Mio had passed. Their expressions had lit with hope—until the first hound had sounded from the castle behind her.

Her family had kept them safe for generations. Mio would not be the first to fail.

"No," Mio said. "There is no other choice."

She slipped her hand into the wide, stiff sash around her waist and pulled out a folded rectangle of leather. Faen's brow rose as she opened it, revealing several slim throwing knives tucked into loops and a larger knife that she'd shoved in the middle.

He let out a whistle. "How did I not feel that when I carried you?"

"My sash is thick enough that this small bundle often goes unnoticed," Mio answered with a shrug.

A smile lit his eyes. "You are a lady of surprises."

"I just wish I had more." Her breath caught as she counted the blades in her pouch. No matter how many times she looked, there were still only seven. Well, eight counting the hunting knife. "Not enough even if I was an expert at throwing them. Which I'm not."

Faen looked over his shoulder at the bow and arrows, then let out a sigh. "We do have the bow. But—" Frowning, Faen stood and moved to the quiver of arrows. "No, not enchanted. He knows well enough that plain arrows won't kill spirit hounds. Typical."

Fighting sudden tears, Mio's hand tightened around the hilt of the larger blade. His father hadn't even cared enough to see him properly armed. "I'm sorry."

"For what?"

Mio lifted her head at the confusion in Faen's voice. "Your father." She took a breath. "For getting you involved. Everything."

Fury closed Faen's throat tight for one long moment. That *she* should be apologizing for his people's failure only surged the anger higher. How could the nobles not see that a Devout stronghold would mean death for many of the *Eiana?* The Devout might call to eliminate magic, but they used creatures of spirit, like the hounds, without compunction. Creatures that could cross between dimensions given enough energy.

Old prejudices would lead the nobles to their doom.

"You have nothing to apologize for." Faen caught her gaze. "Not when your bravery may have saved us."

Her brow wrinkled. "Me? But—"

"You ran to the grove, even knowing you might not be received. My father won't acknowledge it, but your warning has been of great benefit. We'll have some time to prepare for the Devout." He grimaced. "Well, they will. I'll be exiled as soon as we leave this grove."

Lady Mio shoved herself to her feet. "For helping me?"

"In part," he answered. "But more for disobeying. Since I refused to join the ranks of mages, my father has been searching for any excuse to get rid of me."

Her face went pale. "Then you must stay."

Faen picked up the quiver and pulled the arrows free. "No. We'll save many more if we end this threat now."

Closing his eyes, Faen called his meager magic forth. He gritted his teeth as the energy tried to slip free, but he finally forced it into the arrows, tuning them to the spell he needed. Physical weapons could do little against spirit hounds—their bodies weren't true flesh and blood—but

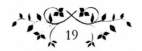

detaching the spirits from the physical realm worked well. A trick his father didn't know about.

As he held his magic firm, he focused on Mio's pinched face. Faen put the arrows back and lifted his free hand. "I'll enchant the knives, if you'll let me."

Though her eyes went wide, she handed him the pouch holding her throwing blades without comment. Muscles trembling with the effort, Faen cast the spell into each knife before returning them. Only then did he let his magic settle back into himself. His knees wobbled, and he fought against the urge to sit. He'd used his power entirely too much for one day.

"Why can't you cast that directly at the hounds?" Mio asked.

Faen glared at the edge of the circle. "I'm not powerful enough to do magic through the barrier. But if I go out there, they'll kill me before I can go through them all."

"Oh." Mio bit her bottom lip. "If we survive this—"

"My lady, I beg you. Make no promises." He kept himself from touching her by dint of will. "Only mages can be noble among my kind. There is nothing I can offer you. Not even an alliance."

"You should listen to him, my bride."

The voice sliced across the clearing, and only training kept Faen from jumping at the sudden sound. As Mio flinched, her face going pale, Faen looked over her shoulder for the source. A tall man stood at the edge of the circle, a cloak much like Mio's falling around him in a splash of color. But no birds woven in for him—pale spirit hounds

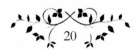

danced on a field of richest purple. That and the hair bound on his head in the Lord's knot told Faen more than enough.

Her step-uncle already claimed victory.

Faen heard Lady Mio take a deep breath as she tucked her pouch of knives back beneath her stiff sash. Then she turned, her shoulders straight and expression blank. "I am not your bride. Nor will I ever be."

"Your mother approved the match."

"At the point of your sword," Mio said. "She is not Lady here. I am. And I have refused your suit."

At a gesture, the spirit hounds gathered around the edges of the man's cloak, looking eerily like they'd just climbed off. "The Devout are coming, Mio. You cannot escape this. Why would you reject my protection?"

Even Faen could sense the fury pouring from the lady, though he wasn't an empath. "Some protection," Faen muttered.

The noble smirked, waving his hand at the empty clearing. "It's more than you can offer, isn't it?"

Faen slung the quiver on his shoulder and bent down for the bow. He took a long breath to calm his fury. Anger made his hands shake, and he needed his aim to be true. "I guess we'll see."

Careful to keep her hunting knife hidden in the folds of her gown, Mio studied her uncle. "Go back north, Kaso. The Lord and Lady of War can never be ascendant."

His eyes narrowed. "Clearly, I disagree."

"What happens once they have destroyed all in their path?" Mio asked softly. "What will the fire do when the wood is consumed?"

"You speak to save yourself," Kaso answered, though something like fear crossed his face. "The Devout have been promised much to rid the world of your kind."

"Light will ever stand firm."

Kaso smirked. "Brave but foolish. It's too bad your blood is tainted. Though it might be worth the risk for the strength of our sons."

A shiver of fear danced down Mio's spine, but she stood firm. "Never."

"We shall see," Kaso said, his voice cold. His looked to the hounds and gave a quick gesture. As one, the spirit hounds sprang for the circle, hitting in one solid line.

Though her grasp of magic was small, the sudden cracking of the spell threw Mio's world askew. Her vision went gray, and behind her, Faen cursed. When she steadied and her vision cleared, she wished it hadn't. The hounds were moving fast, their wicked barks making her heart pound harder as they rushed across the clearing.

Still, she kept her knife hidden.

Arrows rained from behind her right shoulder to thud into the approaching hounds. Three whirled into smoke with ghostly cries. But Faen would never take out the other seven before they reached her. They were just too fast.

Mio lifted a brow. "Can you not enter the circle yourself, Uncle? The Devout must be weaker than they say."

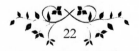

"Why so concerned for me, Mio? Changing your mind?" Kaso asked. But he took a few steps closer.

"I'll wed no man who can't retrieve me himself," Mio answered. Though her voice stayed steady, her hands shook in the folds of her gown. "It would be unworthy."

Two more hounds fell to Faen's arrows before Kaso flicked his hand, sending them toward Faen instead. Mio's breath hitched, but she didn't have time to worry about Faen. Not as Kaso strode forward, his gaze focused on her face. As the last hound rushed past, her step-uncle halted before her.

"Embrace me, Lady," Kaso whispered. "And accept your fate."

"Mio!" she heard Faen gasp from behind her.

But there was only one choice. "Of course."

Kaso opened his arms wide, and Mio moved close, slipping her arms around him at the last moment. Beneath his thick, silk cloak. She took a deep breath and looked into Kaso's eyes as she accepted her fate, for failure would mean death. Lord and Lady of Light give her strength.

A gasp puffed from her lips as she shoved her hand upward, plunging her knife hard toward his back.

Faen perched in a tree once more, thanking every teacher he'd ever had during his training. His speed would save him and Mio both. It *had* to. With the last of the spirit hounds dead, he lifted the bow again, ready to sight on his target. He would only get one chance if he wanted to save Mio. But he

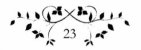

almost dropped his bow instead when he saw that her uncle had already stumbled back.

The other knife. He'd forgotten. Mio clearly hadn't. She stood tall, blood dripping from the tip of the larger blade.

But her uncle still lived, and fury rushed across his face to blend with pain as he reached for Mio. Faen loosed his arrow. It flew true, embedding deep in her uncle's arm. Faen nocked another and prayed Mio would move enough to give him a clear shot. But when she moved, it was closer.

Sunlight gleamed for the briefest moment on the blade she lifted once more.

The smooth hilt slid against Mio's slick palm as she firmed her grip, and her stomach heaved at the thought of his blood on her flesh. But as Kaso's focus shifted to the arrow in his arm, Mio moved. What Faen and the Gods had provided, she would not waste. She lifted her knife and plunged it toward his neck without pausing to think. It sank deep into the soft skin of his throat, and the feel of it…She hardly noticed as her uncle fell hard.

Suddenly, it didn't matter if she lived or died—so long as she could throw up.

Mio felt a hand on her back as she emptied her stomach into the grass, and in that moment, she didn't care who touched her. So long as they kept up that slow, soothing circle. And when she was finished, another hand held out a square of forest-green cloth. Her eyes slipped closed in gratitude as she wiped her mouth, realizing only then that she knelt in the grass.

"You did it," Faen said softly from just behind her.

Mio tensed, jerking to her feet so she could meet his eyes. "I never wanted to take a life, necessary though it was."

"I never thought you did," Faen answered. Pain twisted his expression until he forced it smooth. "I meant only that you saved yourself and my people, too. You have no need of the *Eiana*—or me—now."

Her heart thudded hard in her chest. "That is not true."

"I…" His fists clenched, and his gaze slipped from hers. "I am not a noble, my lady."

"Come with me, and you will be," Mio said, her voice somehow steadier than her hands.

Faen's gaze darted back. "What?"

Gathering her courage, Mio stepped closer—close enough to touch. She lifted her clean hand, stopping a breath away from his cheek. "Wed with me. Be my Lord."

His breath hissed out. "It isn't that easy. So many would—"

"I don't care about anyone else." Mio shivered as her fingers brushed his flesh. "My people will accept you, since your father is noble. Ancestry matters more than magic to the Kioku. But I would choose you even still." She paused, swallowing against the dryness in her mouth. "Will you choose me?"

Faen's eyes searched hers for an eternity, and her throat closed tight. Would this be the last time she touched him, saw him? Then he lifted his own hand to cover hers, pressing her palm against his cheek. His lips curved up, and his eyes went soft. "Always."

CPSIA information can be obtained
at www.ICGtesting.com
Printed in the USA
LVOW11s2328270418
575132LV00002BA/445/P